ME, MYSELF AND I

ON BEHALF OF DEATH, BOOK 8

E.G. STONE

TARNEY BRAE CREATIVE ENDEAVOURS

For the readers of the wild and crazy:
Don't let anyone tell you what to enjoy, just enjoy!

CONTENTS

I don't know if one has to be an expert on sneaking in order to get ready for a trip while also carrying around an Impossibly Dangerous Artefact without any of your office mates noticing, but I imagine it certainly helps. I, apparently, am not an expert at sneaking.

"Ow!" I yelped, clutching my knee where I'd accidentally rammed it into a doorjamb. The bag on my back, carrying a spare pair of clothes, two spare glasses, several bags of coffee beans and a jar with said Impossibly Dangerous Artefact, rattled in a decidedly suspicious manner.

"Going somewhere, Cal?" Agravane leaned against the wall between my office and the stairs up to my flat. He was an aurai, an air elemental, and was possessed of annoyingly attractive features, snark that rivalled my own, and absolutely would not let me get away with as many things as Yolanda.

I debated for a moment, trying to decide whether it

would be wiser to lie as best I could and escape the situation, or whether I should just deny everything and escape the situation. I decided to go with abject denial. "No."

"Liar."

Piffle.

"I am not going somewhere you can go, or should even know about," I amended, straightening my bag and shoving my glasses up my nose.

"Which makes it all the more important that you tell me, so I can prevent you from doing something stupid. Let's face it, Cal, you have a history of rushing headlong into situations which could easily be avoided with a little sense."

I opened my mouth to protest and paused. Considered. Sighed. "You may have a point."

"Good. Now, let's have a seat and you can tell me where you're running off to at three in the afternoon, when you're meant to be working on that marketing campaign for the nymph dancers."

I sighed again and headed back into my flat, Agravane following. We sat on the couch and I pulled the bag off my back, unzipping it to show the aurai the Impossibly Dangerous Artefact. As soon as the jar was revealed, he recoiled, holding a hand over his nose.

"Cal..." he breathed, nose wrinkled, eyes watering. "What *is* that?"

"Death's heart," I said, and knew immediately that I was about to have a companion for my latest quest.

See, my name is Cal Thorpe, and while I was originally

hired to be Death's marketing agent, things became considerably more complicated. It turned out that I was a Grim Reaper, possessed of an eldritch power that let me stand between people at the moment of Life and Death—or at other significant choices in their life. Oh, I also didn't have a soul because Death lost it and therefore couldn't die. Sebastian, what I called my Reaper abilities, warned me that the lack of soul was killing me where nothing else could. This, all parties involved decided, was bad.

Death had told me that the only one who might have an inkling of where my soul was happened to be his mother, a being so impossibly powerful and dangerous that I needed his own heart to get her attention. So he'd pulled it out of his chest and handed it to me, which, as one might expect, had caused a significant amount of anxiety in my life.

Now, carrying around a literal piece of Death in a jar, I was about to head off to the Goblin Market and try to find his mother, all the while avoiding dangerous beings of all sorts that might want the heart. I'd been about to go recruit the djinn, Neja, to help protect me, when Agravane intervened.

Two hours later, after a great deal of panic on both sides of the conversation during which I was forbidden —loudly—from travelling alone, Agravane and I were standing outside of Neja's house. Agravane was heavily armed. I was not.

Really, no one should be stupid enough to put an actual weapon in my hands, no matter what sort of magical artefact I was carrying.

Agravane pounded on Neja's door. "This is a bad idea," he said.

"So you've informed me," I replied. "It's necessary."

"The fewer people involved, the better."

"Yes, well, *you* insisted on knowing what was going on."

This earned me a well-practised glare. He shifted his bandolier of knives and pounded on the door again. It swung open a moment later, revealing Neja wearing ratty old pyjamas, her white hair tangled about her face, dark circles under her eyes and a bottle of some expensive alcohol in her hand.

She took one look at the two of us and let out a string of curses which was actually quite impressive, if entirely unwarranted.

Neja and I had a complicated relationship. She was a bounty hunter and mercenary who would take odd jobs of the dangerous variety for any party in Elsewhere that could afford her rates. We had first met when I was loaned out by Death to the Taxman to collect back taxes. In an unfortunate mix up involving a piano and her wish magic, she'd inadvertently killed me several times. We became friends after that, and had the potential for a great deal more, only my lack of soul and the incredibly terrifying Reaper abilities that lived inside me kept getting in the way. During our last encounter at the coronation party of the rock troll leader, she'd seen what happened when I let my abilities off their leash, and the aftermath had left us both a little wary.

So, perhaps the cursing wasn't entirely unwarranted.

Mostly, but not entirely.

"What are you doing here, Cal?" Neja demanded. She leaned against the door frame and glared at me with far more effectiveness than Agravane had managed. "And how did you know where I live?"

"Death keeps records of such things," I explained. In retrospect, that was not likely a comforting thing. Neja's expression soured further.

I tried to make up for the blunder by finding something else to talk about, at least until she invited Agravane and me inside. The house was nice, cute even, looking more like a pleasant garden cottage than anything I would have expected of Neja. It was situated in a quiet part of Elsewhere and there were no neighbours to bother her, though I had a feeling that the woods her house backed were probably full of very dangerous things. Still, it was nice in a country mouse sort of way.

"Judging my house now, are you?" She was glaring at me in a very pointed manner and I had a feeling that anything I said about her house would not go over well. Still, I needed her to at least tolerate me for this quest and compliments were usually a good way to go.

"It's...cuter than I expected for you," I admitted. "I like the wildflowers."

Neja pointed the bottle of alcohol at me. "Did you just call my house *cute*?"

I nodded. "I rather thought you would live in something with more steel and brick. The country cottage is very nice, though."

"Cal, you should really just shut up while you're ahead," Agravane muttered. I didn't quite understand what was wrong, but did as I was told. In such circumstances, I've learned that Agravane, and my other assistant Yolanda, were much wiser about things that should not be said.

"What, *exactly*, are you two doing here? And armed?" Neja eyed Agravane's many weapons with a wary eye. Given her profession, I suppose I shouldn't have been surprised at her caution, but I had hoped that whatever our personal situation was might earn a little trust.

"I am in need of your help," I said, shifting the backpack so its weight didn't feel quite so ominous. "Please."

Neja blinked, narrowed her eyes at me, studied Agravane for a moment, then finally threw her hands up into the air and stepped aside. "Fine! Why not? Go ahead and ruin an already terrible day!"

I opened my mouth to ask what was so terrible and received an elbow to the side from Agravane. He led us into the house and I was even more astonished by the inside than the out. Mostly because it was in shambles. There were clothes strewn about, papers on just about every flat surface, a large number of knives and swords and things just laying wherever, a strange smell coming from what I assumed was the kitchen, and a weird clicking noise indicating that the radiator had given up and died. Dramatically.

Neja stomped through the debris as if she didn't even notice it, and took another swig of her drink. I tried to be a little more polite and minced my way through the cottage until we got to her sitting room. Neja collapsed onto a couch that was surrounded by various forms of alcoholic detritus—and at least one pizza box—then gestured vaguely towards Agravane and I. We sat on the loveseat across from the couch. I perched the backpack on my lap, not really wanting to put it on the floor.

"So, um…" I started, then looked about. "Did someone break in while we were in the Great Northern Ridge?"

We had got back the day before from the last adventure, and while a great portion of my time had been spent nearly hyperventilating from learning about Death's mother and the fact that I now carried his heart in a jar, I'd at least managed to do laundry.

"No," Neja snapped. "Now, please explain why the last person I wanted to see is in my parlour."

Agravane bared his teeth ferociously. "Are you this rude to all your clients?" he asked, his tone shockingly sweet. Neja scoffed.

"You're here as clients? Not because of the situation with the rock trolls?" she asked. She took another slug of whatever alcohol was in the bottle and chucked the empty container to the side. I winced, overcome by an odd urge to tidy. Or hire a company to do tidying.

"Why would we be here about the situation with the rock trolls? What situation? Did something happen to Yolanda's sister?" I asked. I had left the cheerful Katrina on the throne and basically forcing me into exile after I not-so-accidentally went full Reaper on their former leader, Eddie.

Neja sat up and blinked at me, as if through a drunken haze. She didn't *seem* massively drunk, but I did not know much about how alcohol affected djinns. Mostly, she just seemed unhappy.

"You're not here to force me to keep quiet about your Reaper abilities? To shut me up after what I witnessed?" Neja rasped.

I frowned. "Why would I need you to keep quiet? I'm fairly certain all of Elsewhere knows about what happened by now. It's not like these things stay secret, certainly not after I've rather pushed social media to be the more popular means of sharing news. I will admit, I might not have anticipated the consequences of that particular action, but I was trying to just do marketing for Death, and that is far easier with social media than print adverts and word of mouth these days, especially considering—"

Agravane slapped my shoulder hard enough to jolt me out of my monologue. "Take a breath, Cal," he said.

I did so, then adjusted my glasses. "Apologies."

"Granted," Neja said. She looked confused.

"Why would I need you quiet?" I asked her again, softer this time.

Neja flinched. She wrapped her arms around herself and pulled her knees up. It was the most vulnerable I had ever seen her, and it was probably my fault. I wanted to fix it, and I didn't know how, so I waited for her to answer instead.

"Cal, what I witnessed…it was terrifying. Truly terrifying. I'm a mercenary. A bounty hunter. I have gone after some beings whose power is nearly ancient. And never once have I been as scared as I was than in that cave with you and Eddie. The problem with that sort of power, though, is that it attracts other power. I figured, after everything that went down, you would want things…quiet. So you could gather your forces. Prepare. That sort of thing."

I tried seeing things from her perspective, I really did, but the snort came out of me all the same. "Sorry," I said, then snorted again. "Neja, I'm not laughing at you, I promise."

"Sure seems that way," she snarled.

"No, it's just…I work for *Death*. Any power that wants to get anywhere near him knows they can come after me. I may just be a marketing agent—"

"Hardly *just*," Agravane put in, which was kind, but annoying.

"I'm a marketing agent!" I insisted. "Which means people know about me, know about my clients, know about so very, very many things that I would like to have kept quiet."

"Like the fact that you can't die?" Agravane asked. "Or your coffee obsession? Or the fact that you can't ever get glasses to fit, no matter how they're spelled? Or that situation with the rabbits?"

"Okay, first of all, the rabbit debacle was not my fault!" I complained. "And secondly, my glasses just don't grip my nose. It's a problem with the nose piece that no one can fix. And am not *obsessed* with coffee."

"You're obsessed," Neja said. "It's a well known fact. The subject of many memes. Do you know how many clients have got extra work for sending you baskets of coffee? It's literally the internet's worst kept secret."

"Is that why I keep getting deliveries of coffee?" I asked. "I thought it was just my deal with the brownie who makes it."

"That, too. She's literally one of the richest brownies in Elsewhere, now." Neja had unfolded her arms and was looking a little less concerned. She sighed. "I would love to believe that you don't care about the fact that you're probably one of the most powerful beings in Elsewhere, but it's just…"

"Trust me, Cal cares literally nothing for power. I keep pestering him to do a blog post on the Reality of Reapers, but he just says no." Agravane ruffled my hair and I yelped, smoothing it back down and glaring. "If he wanted power, djinn, do you honestly think that he would be working for Death with only Yolanda and myself as his assistants? I am quite spectacular, yes, but hardly on the calibre of Creatures That Could Destroy Half of Elsewhere."

Neja nodded once. Bit her lip. Then threw a pillow at me. I yelped again.

"I've been worried out of my mind!" she screeched. "I thought you were going to come after me and put a binding spell on me! I thought I was going to have to go into hiding! You couldn't have said you don't care that I know the full extent of your powers? You couldn't have said *something*? You didn't even ask if I was alright!"

I raised a hand. "Considering I only got back yesterday, I haven't had much time to sort out how everyone is doing. I'm still trying to come to terms with things. I know that…" I trailed off, remembering the look that Neja had given me after I had given the rock trolls my ultimatum, after I had offered Eddie a Choice and enforced it with the power Sebastian granted me. She had looked, if not actively afraid, certainly distant. She looked at me like I was someone she didn't know, like every piece of banter we had shared was somehow meaningless in the face of my power. Maybe I didn't care whether I had power or not, but other people certainly did. Neja was one of those people.

I straightened. I was here for a job, not to discuss our nonexistent relationship. "I am here to hire you for a guard position."

Neja blinked and I saw something like disappointment flicker in her gaze before it hardened into the battle-ready djinn I was used to seeing. Nothing fazed her when she was like this. That was what I needed.

"For yourself?" she asked.

I nodded. "I need to go to the Goblin Market and find Death's mother."

Neja's jaw dropped. She sat up so straight I was afraid she'd been electrocuted. Agravane gave her a firm nod. "It's true."

"You can't be serious," she said. "How? Why?"

"I'm dying," I said. I wasn't sure I truly trusted her with that information, not personally, but this was a professional job and I needed her to have all the information to do things properly. So I shoved personal feelings into the void in my mind where my emotions usually vanished and continued. "My Reaper abilities are unstable without the anchor of my soul and I'm fading. If I don't find my soul, I'll become an empty shell and eventually die. Death says the only one who might know where my soul is, is his mother. So we need to find her. He suggested we start at the Goblin Market."

Neja shook her head, then pressed her hands to her hair. "Stars above, Cal, that's seriously dangerous. The Goblin Market is not for the faint of heart on a good day. You'd have to go deep into the market to even get a whiff of Death's mother, and you'd need some sort of beacon to guide you to her. It would attract every dangerous monster from, well, everywhere."

I nodded. "I have a beacon," I said. "But I need guards. While I still cannot be killed, I also can't have this particular beacon falling into anyone else's hands."

Neja nodded, her expression all business now. She flicked her gaze around the room as if cataloguing every weapon she could see. "It'll be dangerous."

"Massively so," Agravane drawled, expression flat. "If you're not up for it—"

Neja held up a hand. "I did not say that. Only that I charge extra for such dangerous work."

Agravane snorted in disgust. "Cal you can't be—"

"Whatever you require, it will be paid," I said. Death's coffers ran deep and I was allowed to dip into them whenever I wanted. A benefit I had used only once, when Agravane had booked the most expensive hotel in Chicago during our business with the Taxman. That had been an accident. This was not.

Neja nodded again, pressing her deep blue lips together. She looked a little feral, and it had little to do with the tangles in her hair or the ratty pyjamas. It was everything to do with the bright spark of magic in her eye. "Very well," she said. "I agree. Now, what is this beacon you're so worried about?"

I unzipped the bag and pulled out the jar. Inside, Death's heart—black, shining with blood that was dark as the void and specked with starlight—beat rhythmically. Neja let out a string of curses that was even more impressive than her first. Then we shook hands. The bargain, whether either one of us liked it or not, was struck.

CHAPTER 2

*I*t turns out that one of the more complicated things about the Goblin Market is actually getting there. The last time I went, while on a quest for Life to help her kill one of her champions—I was acting as Death's proxy; it's a long story—she had just sort of poofed us into the middle of the market. That, apparently, is not the normal way of entry. Not that anything with Life is normal.

"Why are we in Austin, Texas?" I asked, holding up a hand to shield my eyes from the sun. Neja, bathed, dressed, and now possessed of more weapons than Agravane, had arranged for our transport to the mortal realms. Agravane, thankfully, looked just as confused as I felt.

"Why is it so hot?" he grumbled, glaring at the buildings around us. "And why are there so many people? And why—"

"Shut up, you two," Neja snapped. "It's hot because it's summer. There are so many people because it's a city. And yes, the people are weird, because it's Austin. Now, we're looking for The Book Cellar. It's around here somewhere."

We found the book shop a few doors down, behind a wooden door painted a garish shade of red, with a window display of old books that had been sculpted into the shape of a dragon. It was rather impressive, if not entirely accurate. Dragons had far more teeth. Inside the shop, there were shelves of books of all sorts. New on one side, used on another, the selection ranging from the latest political thriller to an entire shelf of indie novels. There were chairs strewn about for the comfort of the customers, and one of them was occupied by a cat whose eyes were disconcertingly intelligent. A man with a scruffy beard and a cheerful green t-shirt sat behind the sales counter, plucking at a mandolin.

"Welcome to the Book Cellar," he said, tone just a shade shy of welcoming. He didn't really look up, just kept playing his instrument, tapping his foot along to some mysterious beat. "How can I help you?"

Neja stepped up to the counter and lay down three silver coins. "We need access to the back alley," she said. The man looked up, giving the three of us the once over, ignored the many weapons on both Agravane and Neja, stared hard at me for a moment, then finally nodded. He looked almost disappointed.

"Alright," he grumbled. He pushed a few buttons on the cash register, deposited the coins, and handed Neja a receipt. "Second door on the left. First one's the bathroom, if you need to stop before you go."

Neja nodded her thanks and we traipsed through the bookstore, deliberately ignoring the large selection of very nice paperback mystery stories and fantasy adventures in favour of the doorway. I suddenly wished that I didn't have to go on this ridiculous adventure. Was it too much to ask for a normal afternoon, just one, before having to run off and perform impossible tasks?

The answer was, as always: apparently, yes.

"Why does no one ever just come in for the books anymore?" the man whined to someone after we had reached the back hallway. The chord he struck on the mandolin was discordant, an exact mirror of his complaint.

"Oh, hush. You're making a profit, right? Just do your job. Besides, you do not want those three lingering in the store. Not with what's in that bag. I can smell it from here, despite the protection spells on the container." The responding voice had a bit of an inherent hiss to it and I wondered, briefly, if it belonged to the cat.

That was silly. That cat was hardly big enough to be a Faerie cat, and those were the only ones that I knew of which could talk. The fact that the voice had identified my Highly Dangerous Artefact was a little concerning, though. I hitched the bag higher on my shoulders.

The second door on the left was painted a vivid red, though this one was more blood and murder than the cheerful welcome of the front door. Neja looked around nervously to see that the coast was clear, then slapped the receipt to the wood. The paper began to glow, then smoke, then dissolved into the paint. The door swung open. A rush of cool air blew over us, bringing with it the smell of far too many people and questionable food.

Without even letting me ask questions, of which I had many, Neja shoved me into the portal. I stumbled and did my best not to fall. Agravane ran into me and we both tripped out of the alleyway that held the entrance to the mortal realms. Immediately, I was hit by a myriad of noises and smells and sights beyond belief. A place of impossibilities, ready to devour its next victim.

The Goblin Market was traditionally a migratory market that never appeared in the same place twice, traversing countries and realms with the ease of powerful magic. In modern times, though, it merely occupied a pocket dimension somewhere between Elsewhere and the mortal realms, connecting to various points by means of portals like the one we'd come through. It looked like a massive underground cave, with the walls made of shining black rock, extending so far overhead that the ceiling was shadowed. Giant stalagmites and stalactites stretched into the air, providing places for carved stone buildings and perches for flying creatures of all sorts. Some of the more permanent shops and buildings were built directly into the walls, with others in tents made of colourful—and probably magical—cloth. There were stalls, wagons, even just a careful nook where someone could set up shop on a rug.

People were shouting out wares and prices and the noise of negotiation was thick in the air. Everyone was selling in the Market and everything was for sale. Literally.

Last time I had come, I was looking for the Iron Witch and was led by Life. It had been a fairly short venture, punctuated only by my discovery of the best coffee ever to have been brewed. This time, I had a feeling I was going to be learning a great deal more about the underbelly of the Market. I wasn't sure that was a good thing.

"Where do we start?" I asked, coughing as a gargoyle walked past, smoking some sort of fragrant herb.

"This is just the fringes of the Market," Agravane said. "Mostly for tourists and day trippers, those who only want a simple bargain, like beauty for years of your life, protection charms, that sort of thing. It's been ages since I've been here. Everything looks so different."

Neja sighed. "The Market is everchanging. That's why I don't like coming here. Things are never the same, and finding what you want to know is ridiculously complicated."

I shifted the rucksack straps. "What about my beacon? Can't we use that?"

"Sure, if you want to draw the attention of everyone within three hundred yards. Only use it when I tell you, okay?" Neja glared at me and I nodded. Twice. "Good. Now, come on. There's a good bar somewhere around here. One of the more permanent fixtures.

There'll be someone there who has the right information."

Then, like a tour guide who was tired of leading gaping tourists about, Neja waved us onward and we traipsed through the market. Either the ridiculous number of weapons borne by Agravane and Neja were enough to keep any casual hawkers away, or I looked like anything but an easy mark. I doubted the latter very much. Still, no one bothered us as we walked towards a stalagmite so large there was an entire high rise carved into it. I did, though, get many, many stares.

"So," I said as we drew closer to the massive rock building. "Is the staring normal?"

"Normal?" Neja scoffed. "This is the Goblin Market. Everything is normal here. However, you are gathering more attention than others, my dear Cal."

"Why?" I brushed down my jacket, wondering if I'd spilled something on it. "Is it my clothes? I tried to dress casually, but I absolutely refuse to wear sweat-pants, and I have the hardest time finding jeans that are as comfortable as wool-silk blend trousers. I suppose I could—"

"It's not your clothes," Neja said, shooting a glare at me. I winced and hunched my shoulders. She was still not happy with me. Great. "It's you. Reaper? Agent of Death? Errand boy to Life?"

"Hey!" I protested. "I am not her errand boy! I am a consultant."

Agravane snorted. "You keep telling yourself that. But I was there when she told you to go pick up her dry cleaning."

"Yes, that was rather demeaning," I admitted. "The cleaners were *not* happy at the state her clothes had been in, and the bill was astronomical. Though, I shouldn't be surprised that Life is hard on her clothes. She does have—"

"Do you *ever* stop talking?!" Neja whirled around and bared her teeth at me. Her eyes flickered with flame and magic. "Stars, Cal, you just—barely—got back on my good side. Don't ruin it with your incessant chatter."

I hunched my shoulders even more. "Sorry," I mumbled. Then, ignoring the look Agravane threw in my direction, I followed Neja without saying anything more. The stares from various people, shop keepers and those walking the narrow lanes alike, continued. I focused my attention on the massive stalagmite before Sebastian could rise to the surface and stare back at the people.

My Reaper abilities were intimidating, to say the very least. It was better to just be as unassuming as possible.

The high-rise we approached was carved in the style of Parisian architecture from the early 20th century, which is to say it was large, grand, very much over the top and intimidating to anyone who approached with less than a fortune to their name. The carvings got more resplendent as they reached upwards, depicting ancient myths from a number of different cultures, all the stories twining together in ways that made very little sense to someone like me. That is to say, the mostly ignorant.

I really hoped the bar was not in this building. I liked the finer things in life, certainly. Bespoke suits were a weakness of mine. But the glitz of this building was beyond me. Thankfully, Neja led us around the back of the building, where we encountered a few steps that led downward, where a few windows were carved into the stone. It was a bar—a pub, actually—that looked as though it had been chipped out of the base of the stalagmite with nothing more than a hammer and chisel. That is, the bar was far from the elegance of the high-rise on the other side. I had the strangest feeling that the bar was older. Much, much older.

Neja knocked on the door and it swung open to reveal an ogre that barely fit into the frame. "Hey, Steve," Neja said. "Got a couple of clients looking for a good time."

The ogre looked us over, frowning at Agravane and practically glowering at me. I waved, trying to smile cheerfully.

"What have we told you about smiling, Cal?" Agravane hissed in my ear.

"Don't do it?"

"Precisely."

I sighed and shoved my hands into my pockets, trying my best to look unassuming. You would think with my being human, and an average one at that, unassuming would be no problem. Apparently, I had developed a reputation. I would have to work on that.

"The aurai can enter," the ogre said. "The Reaper stays out."

"Hey!" I protested.

Neja elbowed me in the ribs. I coughed. She put her hands on her hips and lifted her chin to stare Steve down, which was quite the feat given she was literally half his height. "The Reaper is paying my bills, buddy. He comes."

"She doesn't want trouble," Steve grumbled. "Last time—"

"Last time," Neja said with a dismissive wave of her hands, "I was hired by some idiotic elementals who thought that they oozed class and wealth. They were wrong. I made sure they paid damages. This is entirely different."

The ogre raised one very large eyebrow. "Different how?"

"This is Cal." Neja slung one arm around my shoulder and pulled me forward. "He is a Reaper, yes, but he is also completely harmless unless provoked. Like, literally can't even manage to stab someone if you hand him a knife and put a target right in front of him."

I stiffened. Turned to glare at Agravane. "It was *one* time."

"Cal, we gave up on teaching you any fighting immediately afterward. Just accept the truth and move on." Agravane clapped my shoulder in a friendly manner and beamed up at the ogre.

Steve watched this with a discerning eye, his glower firmly in place. Then he nodded. "I will ask."

The door slammed in my face before I could even ask who he was going to ask. A minute later and the door swung open again, this time revealing a woman with skin patterned like a python or boa constrictor or some sort of jungle snake. She had no hair and her eyes were wide, eager and red. Her lips matched her eyes, and when she smiled, needle-like fangs showed. That was all fine and dandy, but what really got me was that instead of legs, she had coils.

I never really liked snakes much. Especially not when they looked at me like I was dinner.

"A Reaper," she purred, leaning one arm against the door frame and propping the other on her hip. "In my little establishment. My, my, I *am* moving up in the world."

"Sabine," Neja said, one hand resting on her hip relatively close to the hilt of a knife. "We'd like to come in. Have a drink. Maybe ask some questions. No trouble."

Sabine laughed, the sound unnatural. I blinked and wondered whether to describe it as hissing when it sounded more like a drunk sorority girl from the soap operas Agravane and Yolanda were fond of. I decided not to say anything.

"Trouble? Who said anything about trouble? No, I am perfectly happy to grant you entry, under one condition." Her smile turned almost predatory.

"Condition?" Agravane asked. He did not sound pleased.

"That's how things work in the Market, my dear aurai. A service for a price. Always." The snake woman turned to fix me directly in her gaze and I wished I was one of those people who could come up with clever remarks on the spot. "My price is simple. You must participate in tonight's entertainment."

"Entertainment?" I squeaked. I really hated being involved in entertainment. Especially when I was certain it would involve some sort of bloodsport that I would fail epically at, then would die, several times. I really, really hated dying. It hurt. A lot.

"Oh, yes. It's karaoke night. And the whole thing is going to be live streamed."

I was wrong. I really, really wanted bloodsport.

CHAPTER 3

"I can't sing," I hissed under my breath. We were sitting at a small table relatively central to the bar—and make no mistake, this place was a bar, despite its pub-like looks, complete with sticky floor, unfortunate nut-related snacks in bowls around the room, and the aroma of despair that came from late night escapades with cheap alcohol. Neja had sent Agravane off for drinks, unwilling to either leave me alone or trust me with the drinks order. I hadn't yet decided which.

"It doesn't matter if you can sing," Neja said, glaring at a tiny goblin-like thing that was eyeing my rucksack with a glint in its eye. "Sabine only wants entertainment. It's good marketing, Cal. You should know that."

"I am well aware of the tactics that people will go to for marketing," I sniffed. "It *is* my job, after all. I just… prefer being on the other side of the marketing scheme."

"Yeah, well, get over it, Reaper. You're a Big Deal now and that means if people can use you to raise their own star, they will. You're doing karaoke."

I was tempted to bury my head in my arms on the table, but as I wasn't sure when the thing had last been cleaned, I settled for a dramatic sigh. "Don't say I didn't warn you."

Agravane returned a moment later, drinks in hand. He gave a pint of what appeared to be lager to Neja, held on to a glass of red wine for himself, and deposited a glass of what was definitely *not* coffee before me. I stared at it.

"It's a gin and tonic," Agravane said. He took a sip of his wine and winced.

"But…coffee?" I asked.

"Deal with it, Cal," Agravane grumbled. "This is what you get for ordering coffee at a bar. A bad bar, at that."

Neja snorted. "Do you honestly think people come here for the booze? No. This place is practically the centre for information trading in the Goblin Market. You can find out just about anything here. That's why it is so pricey to get in. Sabine knows exactly what goes on here and makes a tidy profit."

I stared despondently into my drink. Sebastian, though, was very interested in the G and T. I gave in, letting the Reaper half of me revel in what was really a very bad glass of mostly tonic water. I coughed. "That's *awful*."

"In-for-ma-tion," Neja chanted. "Honestly, Cal,

weren't you listening? People don't come here for the drinks!"

"Yes, well, if you're going to be the centre for information trading, you might as well have good drinks," I groused. "So, who are we here to talk with?"

I looked around. For such a terrible establishment, it was full to the rafters with people. There were people of just about every kind in the place, and most of them looked quite respectable. Only a few looked like the sort to drag you into a back alley and steal your wallet. Most of those were the bouncers. The only problem was, there were so many people that I had absolutely no idea who it was that would have information on where to find Death's mother.

The slightly transparent spirits in the back corner? Or the ghouls they were haggling with? Perhaps it was the small man with the very large hat juggling—literally—glasses of whiskey. Or even the things by the bathrooms that looked more like zombies that had lost a battle with a hoover.

There were too many options to count. Also, I really needed to get better about learning the various species of magical creatures.

"No idea," Neja said. "If I had that sort of information, don't you think we'd be out of here by now? No, we have to wait for the right person to find us."

"And how, exactly, are they meant to do that?" Agravane asked. He was looking extra grumpy, perhaps because the wine was really terrible. Or he hated karaoke just as much as I did.

"This is the Goblin Market," Neja said, taking a long draught of her drink. "I have absolutely no idea how it works. It just does."

Great. A semi-sentient magical market. Just what we needed.

Before I could say something to that effect, the already-dim lights in the bar dimmed even more and Sabine slithered out onto the raised platform that was the stage. Several spotlights flared to life and the woman was made all the more terrifying because of it. She grinned and bared her teeth in what would loosely be called a smile.

"Good evening, dear friends and patrons," she said in a smooth voice designed to lure in people like me to terrible entertainment schemes. "I would like to welcome you to my humble bar. Tonight, we have a special event planned, one which I think you will quite enjoy. In place of our usual guest band, and by popular demand, we will have our first karaoke night. So warm up your singing voices!"

Then, terror of terrors, she turned her eyes to me. "Our first participant, the one who will launch us into the evening, is someone you have all heard of, but likely thought—or hoped—never to meet. Death's agent and Life's advocate, don't let his unassuming front fool you. He is danger itself. I present to you, the Grim Reaper!"

Two of the spotlights flew around the room to land on me. I was entirely unprepared for the sudden atten-tion and blinked rapidly while blindly reaching for my drink. I downed the gin and tonic as quickly as possible, then reached for Agravane's undrunk glass of wine and downed that, too. I was reaching for Neja's lager when she slapped my hand away.

"What are you doing, Cal?" she muttered.

"Trying to get drunk!"

Agravane snorted. "You can't get drunk. Remember? Side effect of having no soul? Think of all those times we've tried, how much fun we had?"

I remembered, unfortunately. I had a very large number of pictures on my phone with Yolanda and Agravane in various states of inebriation with me in the middle, looking thoroughly unimpressed. They had become a rather popular meme here in Elsewhere, and it was more than a little embarrassing.

In this moment, though, it was just horrifying. "I can try! Oh, this is going to be terrible. Really, truly awful. I mean, you've never heard me sing for a very good reason. I don't even hum in the shower!"

Neja refused to listen to any more of my desperate arguments. She stood from the chair, wrapped a hand around my arm and bodily dragged me to the stage. I was pulled up the rest of the way by Sabine, who wrapped her arm around me. Sebastian, who had been sleeping soundly inside me, despite my panic, now lifted its head and glared at the woman. She seemed undeterred, though I saw her pupils narrowing.

"What sort of song shall we do, Reaper? A pop tune? Folk? Rock? What sort of music does the big bad Grim Reaper listen to?" She was speaking close to my ear, almost intimately, but there was no doubt that everyone in the bar could hear her clearly. I really hated being on this side of the marketing schemes.

"I, ah, prefer classical music," I said. Sabine laughed.

"Classical! How quaint. What elvish ballads do you know? I'm sure we'd love to hear you sing one of those."

Curses. I straightened my jacket. "Human classical music. I'm not very good with music from Elsewhere, yet."

"Oh, very well." Sabine raised a hand and a floating list of music appeared before me. I reached for it and was immediately dismayed when I read the options. Classical apparently did not mean the same thing in Elsewhere as it did in the mortal realms.

For example: Beethoven's 9th symphony—in German—was listed directly above Pink Floyd's *Us and Them*. I scanned the list for something, anything, that I could sing that would remotely resemble music. Then, I saw *the* song.

"That one." I pointed.

Sabine raised a brow. "Interesting choice. But very well. It will make for good livestreaming."

I doubted it, given how poorly I sang, but if that's what she wanted to believe, then so be it. She waved her hand again and a floating scroll with lyrics appeared just above the heads of the crowd, who were all watching me with bated breath. Sabine grinned at me, then slithered away. I gulped. Audibly.

I reminded myself that I was doing this because I really didn't want to fade away into the nothingness that awaited me if I didn't find my soul. I needed to find Death's mother so she could point me in the proper direction. I needed to get my soul back if I wanted to continue existing. Which, by the way, I did.

A little public humiliation had to be worth it.

Then, music began playing from who knows where and I screwed my eyes closed, taking a deep breath. Before I could question the sanity of what I was about to do, I started to sing, off-key, to "The Monster Mash."

It was as terrible as you might think.

I did my best to forget about the audience and focus on the lyrics and the fact that I needed to do this to find my soul. And I did my very best to not listen to any of the sounds coming out of my mouth. Because I'm sure they were akin to a dying possum on helium.

As expected, there was no applause at the end of the song. Sabine slithered out onto the stage, her mouth gaping, eyes wide. If she could look more concerned, it would be an impossible feat of nature.

"I, ah…thank you, Reaper, for that…contribution to our karaoke night. We will be sure to never, ever have you do that again." She let out a weak laugh and there were a few answering echoes in the crowd.

"I warned you," I said. "I can't sing."

"You were not lying," she admitted. "I thought you just wanted to avoid embarrassment. But that was truly atrocious."

"Oh, I'm really bad at lying. Can't keep the stories straight. Really bad at poker, too." With that non sequitur, I handed her the list of songs and climbed off the stage. Neja and Agravane were at the table, Neja looking at me like I'd just pulled out some really dangerous weapon and was brandishing it about for no good reason. Agravane had his head buried in his arms. I think he was laughing.

"Cal," Neja said, drawing out the syllable of my name like a warning. "I don't even know how to…that was…we will never speak of this again."

"Agreed," I said. Agravane leaned back in his chair and wiped tears from his eyes.

"Yolanda would have been appalled! That was the worst thing I've ever heard."

"What *don't* you understand about never mentioning this again?" I grumbled. A kindly pixie of some sort dropped off another gin and tonic at the table, giving me a wince and muttering something about "on the house." Some other unfortunate fools took to the stage, launching into a rendition of some folksy ballad that was actually decent. The tension in the air relaxed and the crowd finally looked away from me.

We sat there in relative silence, ignoring each other while a few more brave people went and sang their hearts out. None were as terrible as me, which was a relief. Then, just as I was about to finish my third drink, a large, hulking figure dragged over a chair and sat at our table.

The guy looked like a barbarian from some bad television show from the 90s. Long, lanky hair, a plethora of leather and studs, a glower that could curdle milk and a jaw that was distinctly crooked. When he spoke, though, he was all elegance.

"I hear that you are seeking information on the

darker corners of the Market," he said. He pulled out a flask and poured a large dose of amber liquid into an empty glass.

"We are looking for something closer to ancient than dark," Neja said, refusing when he offered her the flask. "Anything can find shadows. But it's far more difficult to find things that have been forgotten."

They were talking in riddles and I had no idea what was going on. I comforted myself by the fact that Agravane also looked confused. Or at least disappointed that the stranger didn't offer him the flask.

"These days, they're much the same." The stranger eyed Neja, lip curled. Then, he turned to me.

"Reaper," he said in a low tone. "I know what you're looking for."

"Do you?" I asked, surprised. I was rather hoping that the wheels of gossip hadn't got around to working just yet. After all, Death had given me his heart when we were alone, and I hadn't shown anyone other than Agravane and Neja. Though the voice in the bookstore had identified the item, and who knew how many others could smell the raw power coming off the thing.

"One such as you would not be seeking such paltry things as gold or exotic spices or immortality," the man said. He took a healthy sip of his drink. "No, you seek something far more…elusive."

"Oh?" I was beginning to think this guy was a charlatan, looking for a quick payout from people who were too gullible to know better. Until, that is, he looked me right in the eye and said the exact words that would have sent my skin shivering had I been at all emotionally aware.

"You seek power. An audience with Fate herself. Get an audience with her, and all the realms are at your feet."

Neja and Agravane became very still. I shoved my glasses up my nose.

"You make it sound as though you know precisely where I can find Fate, and not only that, but you make it sound easy," I said, trying to sound bored. It was, apparently, one of the few tones I could manage with ease. At least, according to Yolanda it was. "I may be human, but I'm not an idiot. There is some sort of catch. Either that or your price is ridiculously high."

At the mention of price, the barbarian with the eloquent tongue stiffened. His eyes flashed to either side, but the audience was entranced by the karaoke. Either that, or they were wise to the ways of the Goblin Market and knew better than to listen in to private conversations in a way that could be easily noticed.

I really hoped Neja knew what she was doing, bringing us here.

"The path to Fate is straightforward," the stranger said. "Just incredibly dangerous."

"So, business as usual, then," I said. I sighed. "Are you going to continue wasting my time? I could be drinking a cup of coffee right now, not some poor excuse for a cocktail. If you're not going to be useful, then I have better things to do."

I went so far as to push my chair back from the table

before the stranger reached out and grabbed my hand. Immediately, Sebastian became alert, focusing its attention on the man. I did the same. Whatever it was that people saw when they looked at me as a Reaper was enough to make most people cower in fear, and that was when my powers weren't fully manifested. This man, for all his size and charisma, was no different. He froze, eyes wide. Then, slowly, he withdrew his hand.

Neja let out a quiet snort. The sound sent Sebastian back into watchful slumber.

I waited a few beats for the stranger to speak.

I was not disappointed.

"I can direct you to where the path begins," he breathed. "But no further."

"And your price?" I asked.

"I want an audience with Life." These words were spoken so quietly that I barely heard them, and if anyone else in the bar heard them, then they weren't letting on. I was a little surprised, though. That was hardly much of an issue for me. I could get an audience with Life by merely wishing that she would stay away from me; she was bothersome like that. Then again, I did work for Death and was contracted out to her for odd jobs. I imagine it was a little more complicated for regular people.

"Alright, then," I said. Neja and Agravane looked at me with alarm. "I'll have to set up an appointment, mind you. And I can only guarantee you a few minutes, as she's rather, ah, flighty. But give me your contact information and I'll email you."

The stranger stared at me. "That's it? You just… agree like that? No negotiation?"

I chuckled. "You want an audience with Life? Very well. You want to admire her or fight her or anything at all? You are more than welcome to try. But I can guarantee that Life will not bow to your wishes any more than she bows to Death's. Still, I agreed to get you an audience. The rest of whatever your scheme is, well, that's up to you."

I held out my hand and the stranger shook it without hesitation. There was some sort of tingle that went up my arm, like a mild electric shock. I flinched.

"Market magic," Neja supplied as I looked to her in question. "It will make sure you keep your bargain."

I hadn't planned on backing out, but it was encouraging to know that I was now bound by magic to keep my word. I handed over my phone and the stranger fumbled through putting his contact information in, his thumbs far too large for the screen. Then, with a nod, he leaned in close, looked furtively around, and spoke without moving his lips.

"Fate can be found beyond the resting place of the doomed."

With that, the man pushed away from the table and fled the bar. I looked at my phone. He had entered: Baldwin the Gargantuan.

"Marvellous," I said drily, shoving my phone away. "We just got directions from a man who refers to himself as 'The Gargantuan.' If that's not a bad sign, I don't know what is."

Neja and Agravane both stared at me, exchanged a glance, then stared at me again.

"What?" I asked.

"The resting place of the doomed?" Neja hunched her shoulders. "No one comes out of there in one piece. Ever."

I sighed. "Then can we at least go somewhere with a decent drink before we go to get eviscerated?"

CHAPTER 4

$\mathcal{O}$ne of the problems with trying to traverse the Goblin Market was that it was shifting constantly. Those buildings and shops that were not literally carved into the stone moved with abandon. Some had legs that marched in a steady rhythm from here to there. Others just vanished, then reappeared somewhere entirely different. The rest were actively packed up and relocated based on whims that were as unpredictable as Life.

Basically, finding one's way around the Market was nearly impossible without help. And I'd only been here about an hour. There was no way I'd be of any help even trying to navigate to the loo.

Neja, though, knew where we were going, but wasn't quite certain how to get there. So we stopped, often, asking for directions for the price of a selfie or a coin or some coffee. Nothing so expensive as an audience with Life, nor anything so revealing as people wanting to be acknowledged by the Reaper. Just tiny things that made up the base of commerce here.

But the farther we went, the less friendly the Market became. Stalls selling cheerful things like bottled light or the whisper of waves or protection charms made way for places that sold impossibly sharp knives, cloaks that captured darkness, creatures bred specifically for protection, and far worse. The customers became shifty-eyed, the sellers cunning.

After a while, Neja no longer had to ask for directions.

"Is it meant to be this dark?" Agravane muttered as we neared a collection of small ramshackle buildings that looked like an abandoned movie set from a Wild West film.

"Don't ask questions," Neja snapped. I was about to ask why when she flicked her arm out towards me, a knife pointed at my throat. It wouldn't kill me, but I got the message all the same. "Seriously, Cal. No questions. This place is dangerous for the overly curious. There are things here that will answer your questions and then exact their price for the answer in a variety of unpleasant ways. They feed on fear and despair of the innocent."

I opened my mouth again and the knife dug in a little more.

"No. Questions." Neja sheathed her knife again and I made a show of keeping my mouth shut. Agravane shot me a look and I shrugged.

Sebastian turned over inside me, those eldritch coils tightening and loosening in what felt like a stretch, preparing for whatever was out there, watching. The back of my neck prickled.

The buildings around us seemed to loom the farther into this place we went. There were a few creatures about, some sitting in rickety old chairs on porches, others dragging carts through the lanes. I recognised none of the creatures, and could not even begin to guess what they were. Some had four arms, others hinged legs like animals. All of them eyed the three of us like we were a meal.

"In there," Neja said, pointing to a corner building with swinging doors. "The only way to the resting place of the doomed is through there. It's a gaming establishment. Don't sit down to a game. Don't take any bets. Don't offer any bets. We want to get in and out as quickly as possible."

"Understood," Agravane said, voice as serious as I'd ever heard him. He looked wary and his fingers were twitching towards his bandolier more than in previous sections of the Market.

"Very well," I said. "I'm terrible at gambling, anyways."

Both Neja and Agravane shot me a look. I shrugged. It was true. The only game of poker I'd ever won had been because Al Capone cheated so that he would lose. It's a long story. Otherwise, I was a really terrible gambler. I could even lose at Go Fish on a consistent basis.

The gaming establishment looked an awful lot like a stereotypical movie saloon. There were wooden tables strewn about haphazardly, a bar in one corner stocked with what looked to be primarily whiskey, several people with dark, homespun clothes and large hats, and many, many pictures on the wall done in black and white or faded sepia.

"I've walked into a film," I said, looking about. "Some strange mashup between a Spaghetti Western and a sci-fi horror piece. It's bizarre."

"Cal, shut up," Agravane hissed. I did as he told because Sebastian was suddenly awake and looking about with interest, not because all the patrons had turned to stare at me with varying levels of dangerous intent.

Neja grabbed my arm and dragged me through the saloon to the bar. A stick-thin creature that looked to be actually made of wood propped an elbow on the bar and regarded us with open curiosity.

"You'll be wanting something, I expect," they said with a voice like the cracking of twigs. Neja clapped a hand over my mouth before I could say something.

"We need to go out back," she said. The bartender reeled backwards with a clicking sound that was remarkably distressed.

"You want me to open the gateway." It was definitely not a question, with those icy tones of accusation. Neja just nodded. She looked resigned, even a little sad. Sebastian let out a low growl. I mentally hushed my Reaper abilities and tried not to do or say anything stupid. I had no idea what this gateway was, but the way that everyone in the place suddenly became very keen on cashing out of their card games and shuffling towards the door was suggestive.

"The gateway is dangerous," the bartender said, also eyeing the fleeing patrons. "No sane person would want to open it. And the insane can't afford it."

I leaned on the bar. "I can't tell you which category I fall into, but I can assure you that I can afford it. Whatever the price is."

"Cal," Agravane warned. I held up a finger, cutting him off.

"This is personal, Agravane. I intend to see this through, no matter the cost. If you wish to turn back, then do so. I will not think any less of you." And I wouldn't. It was a simple fact that some people were capable of stepping into danger and others were not. Agravane had already fled the Order of Silence, a group of assassins that were trained by experiencing various levels of torture. He had helped me immensely on the occasion of sorting out a tax problem in Chicago, but the danger there was primarily to me. As I intended it to be here. That didn't mean this would not spill over. If he did not want that, I would not stop him from leaving.

I wished I could turn away, too.

"I'm with you," he breathed. "Whatever it means."

I nodded. Neja watched this with her mouth drawn into a flat line, then she nodded, too.

The bartender let out another one of those clicking sounds then gestured to a door on the far wall. "Come with me," they said and loped off. We crowded around the door while the bartender fumbled with the handle. The door opened into a small storage closet with a further door beyond. This one looked to be carved out of stone with a symbol in the centre that was a collection of squiggly black lines. It was obviously important, given the sharp breath from Agravane and the determined silence from Neja, but it meant nothing to me.

"You must be sure about this," the bartender said. I nodded. "Very well. My price, then, Reaper, is that when you go through this door, you turn to look back. Just once."

"You want me to—"

"No questions, Cal," Neja reminded me. She looked ill.

"Yes," the bartender said with a firm nod. "Look back. That is all."

"Very well," I said. "I will look back."

The bartender looked relieved. It nodded again, then stretched out a hand and pressed it against the symbol of black lines. Then, the bartender spoke again and I began to understand the reason why this place, whatever it was, allowed no questions.

"Do you wish to step through the gate?"

As soon as the question was spoken, a baying howl set up outside, like a horde of creatures with murder in mind ran this way. The bartender looked to me with raised brows. They had gone a little pale, the lines in its skin like that of a dying tree.

"I wish to step through the gate," I said, the words falling out of my mouth like stones, creating ripples as they landed. Each one struck the bartender, making them flinch.

"Do you wish to step through the gate?" they asked again. The howling grew louder, becoming interspersed with growls and the sound of tearing walls. Whatever it was that sought questioners was coming into the saloon by any means necessary.

"I wish to step through the gate." This time, my words were slow, deliberate. Sebastian lifted its head and bared its teeth at whatever was back in the saloon.

"Do you wish to step through the gate?" The third time was what held the magic. I could feel it in the way the door shivered, the symbol below the creature's hand pulsating with ferocious intent.

"I wish to step through the gate," I whispered, Sebastian's voice mingling with mine, matching the gate power for power.

With a tremendous crack, the stone door split evenly in half, the pieces falling sideways and leaving nothing but emptiness in their place. The bartender shivered and fell to the floor, cradling their hand in their lap. The limb was withered and dead, skin sloughing off and rotting away as I watched. They nodded at me.

"Go, Reaper."

Neja wasted no time, shoving Agravane through before he could say something or do anything other than go through the gate. I could feel the power that held it open receding even as I stood there. The bartender nodded again. Sebastian let out an urgent hiss. I went.

Then, to fulfil my promise, I paused with one foot on the threshold and one foot beyond, and looked back.

I knew, then, why the creature had asked this price

of me. Not to see what I had wrought with my request; no, this thing had likely guarded the gateway for ages and knew the ending that would come. No, this thing, this creature for whom I had no name, wanted me to remember their face before they was torn apart by living shadows come to stop whoever was trying to go through the gate. Their tree bark skin shredded easily beneath dark claws. The fangs of the monsters met little resistance in tearing at their limbs. The monsters slavered and bayed, and were only delayed in reaching for me by the body of the creature who lay before the gate. The one who had asked me to look back, so that they would be remembered. Their eyes met mine as they died, a tiny sliver of gratitude all that remained there. I would surely never forget.

I turned around again and stepped all the way through the gate. There was no pull of magic, no sound to indicate that I had stepped through a portal, nothing. One minute I was in the storage closet about to be torn apart by monsters, the next, I was in a misty graveyard with headstones that had seen better days. The ground was mostly dirt with the occasional weed or tuft of grass. There were no flowers on these graves, no indication that anyone had been here at all.

Behind me, there was no portal, no opening, no fence even. Just more graveyard. I could vaguely make out the shape of massive stalagmites and stalactites in the distance, and the sky was solid enough to be stone as well. We were still in the Goblin Market, but well beyond any place that other people visited.

It was empty. Quiet. Peaceful even.

After the destruction I had just witnessed, it felt wrong.

"The guardian of the gateway?" Agravane asked, not quite meeting my gaze.

"Dead," I said. "It was a choice, made long ago. I could feel that much, at least."

"But we caused it, Cal." My junior marketing agent —and friend—had a front to show the world that was quite effective: arrogant, attractive, above the petty things that mere normal people worried about. But I'd also seen him weep after a beloved character on a soap opera died. I'd seen the terror in his eyes before I freed him from the Order of Silence. Now, he looked ashamed.

"I caused it, if you must find someone to blame," I said, resting a hand on his shoulder. "But that death was inevitable, just as it was a choice. They wanted me to turn back to remember them at the end. Not to feel guilty."

"You can try to justify this all you like, but it's not that simple," Neja put in. She, too, looked distinctly uncomfortable, though her expression read more as anger to me than shame. Anger that was likely directed at me. "Your quest killed a good and ancient creature."

"Was there another way to get here?" I asked, gesturing to the graveyard.

Neja scuffed her heel on the ground and studied the nearest headstone. "Not a fast one," she whispered. I said nothing. There was no need to rub salt in her wounds. She had brought us here, and by her own admission there was another path we could have taken, even if it was impossibly slow. I, though, had been the cause of the bartender's death. I knew this. I accepted it. I doubted Neja would ever see it that way.

I looked around a bit more, ready to change the subject. Mist swirled at our feet, brushing up against the headstones like a cat. "I didn't expect the resting place of the doomed to be quite so…literal."

"This is just the entrance, where they put the bodies of people stupid enough to come here," Neja said. She nodded towards the stone wall that was surrounding the place. "There should be a path through there. Come on."

We walked. The headstones loomed taller the closer we got to the wall, the script detailing the names and stories of the dead becoming more and more ancient and obscure. I had never done well with ancient languages at school and university, but I recognised a few as Greek and Sumerian cuneiform.

"So, what exactly is the resting place of the doomed?" I asked, stepping over a plant that was trying its hardest to grow. "Besides a really creepy name, that is."

"I've only heard stories," Agravane said, giving a shrug. "Mostly about really, really old monsters. Tests, sometimes, like they would give to heroes of old. Riddles and errands and such."

"It's as good a description as any," Neja said. She was fingering her knives again. "It's a place where inevitability rules. That's why there are so many dead, because Death is inevitable. They would send heroes and would-be-heroes here to test there mettle. The theory was that if it were inevitable that they were to achieve greatness, then these tests would be easy for them to pass. Everyone else was to succumb to the inevitability of their doom. That is, failure due to arrogance and pride. People also call it the Path of Fools."

I didn't have anything to say to that, except, "Neja, maybe you and Agravane should stay behind, then. After all, I'm still basically immortal, even if I am fading away. I don't want you to…"

I trailed off. Neja paused and looked at me over her shoulder. There was still anger in her eyes, but it was softer now, mixed with something more compassionate. She sighed and shook her head. "I would really love to dislike you, Cal. You keep getting me into bad situations. But you're just so…"

"Naïve? Oblivious? Idiotic?" Agravane asked, his voice pitched in forced cheer. "I could go on. The list is very long."

"Stupidly selfless," Neja finished. She looked me over, gave a firm nod and started walking again.

I blinked a few times. Shoved my glasses up my nose. Thought about it. If I could blush, I'm sure I would have, but my outward emotional responses were consistently muted. "Thank you," I said, and found that my voice was a croak.

Neja waved a dismissive hand and stalked onwards. I hurried to catch up.

"I was serious," I said. "You two could stay behind."

"This is your quest, Cal," Neja said. "Agravane and I are bodyguards, freelancers. This place won't bother much with us."

I had a feeling that her statement was more hope than anything else, but I decided to say nothing. I might have been incredibly incompetent at anything resembling fighting, but I would do what I could to keep those two safe. It wouldn't be fair if they died on my behalf. Not that Life was much for fairness. And Death did not care if you died by means of a fork in a wall socket, or saving thousands of orphans from a rockslide. I shook my head; my thoughts were becoming depressing, even for me.

Finally, we reached the wall of stone. The air was, if possible, quieter than before. There was no hint of movement, not even a breath of wind to move the mist along. The stone before us was tall and smooth, and I didn't really fancy trying to scale it to get to the next part of this ridiculous quest.

"We'd better find a gate," I said. "Right or left?"

"Straight," Agravane said. He jerked his head to the wall, which was now shimmering and rippling. It was disturbing to watch, like witnessing an earthquake, only on a wall. The shimmering abated and the stone stopped shaking, revealing a rough outline of a door. There was even a knocker in the centre of the wall in the shape of a sleeping giant resting his head on mountains. I hoped there wouldn't be giants beyond this wall. They held a grudge. I knocked.

There was a crack and the seams of the stone door split, leaving a slab of solid rock falling directly towards me. Luckily, I had the reflexes of a terrified mouse and scurried out of the way just in time. Neja and Agravane stood off to one side, eyes wide.

"I guess the test has started," I said, peering down at the stone door, which had done its very best to squish me. "Doesn't seem sporting to start before I've entered."

"Yes, because I'm sure this place cares about being sporting," Neja said, voice high.

"Shall I go first, then?" I asked, pointing at the hole in the wall. When no one answered, I shifted the pack tighter on my back and stepped through the wall. When I didn't immediately get impaled or disembowelled or anything, I took a chance and looked around.

I stood in the middle of a forest. Not just any forest, but an English forest. The trees were tall, old, mostly hardwood, and had leaves of bright green that fluttered gracefully against the sky. That, thankfully, was still dark as stone and dripping with stalactites. The ground was not choked with undergrowth, but almost cultivated and tidy, everything covered with a layer of dead leaves. There was even a certain amount of light that filtered through the trunks of the trees, though it wasn't quite the same as a sunny day.

"I'm not dead," I offered to Neja and Agravane. "That is, no one has tried to kill me."

Why would we want to kill you, young hero? Voices rippled through the leaves like whispers upon whispers, eager and hungry. *It has been generations of mortal beings since we last had a hero upon whom to whet our appetite. We wish to see what you will do, human. How you will cower in fear before the tests we have prepared. How you will weep and beg for mercy. How you will scream. Then, when your emotions have filled our bellies, then we will kill you.*

I wanted to say, "Good luck with that." I wanted to explain that I was not really able to feel most emotions, and those that I could were erratic and mostly to do with coffee, so scaring me would probably not taste as good as they would like. I didn't get to say this, or ask who the whispers belonged to. Before I could utter so much as a single syllable, there was a *pop* and the air felt suddenly still.

I looked around. The trees had stopped swaying in their imaginary breeze. The pleasant cultivated forest was now imposing and akin to something one might find in a horror film. I turned back to tell Neja and Agravane to wait a moment, but they were gone.

"Bother," I said. Sebastian lifted its head and growled agreement.

I turned back to the forest. "I do believe you've kidnapped my friends."

We have, the whispers said with glee.

"That was rather stupid of you."

What will you do, human? They were taunting me, I was sure of it.

I was about to start spouting some ridiculously violent things, just to see if I could rattle the whispers and trick them into giving me a clue as to where they'd taken my friends, but in the second time within the span of a minute, I was unable to say anything. This time, though, it was because something smallish, winged, and very, very familiar barrelled into my stomach at full speed.

CHAPTER 5

I don't know if you've ever been rammed in the stomach by a very fast-moving object of approximate cat size, but let me tell you that it is extremely uncomfortable. My organs squished, I lost my balance, flailed, fell, and only *barely* managed to avoid crushing the rucksack beneath me. I groaned in pain.

When I could feel something other than agony, I sat up and looked at the thing that had attacked me.

"T-tempest?" I stammered.

The creature let out a cry of joy and launched at me again. I managed to catch it in my arms this time, and I brought it to me in a hug. I didn't know how it was possible, but it was Tempest, though blue and slightly translucent. Tempest was a miniature griffin that had bonded to me during my journey to the Great Northern Ridge Tribe. She'd been a fascinating mix of barn owl and nearly black cat with just a hint of striping. She'd also enjoyed perching on my head. Unfortunately, she'd been killed by Yolanda's cousin Eddie while he tried to escape after attempting to rile his people into war. That act had caused my Reaper abilities to manifest, which led to a whole slew of other problems.

I'd been devastated at her loss.

But now she was here. I didn't know how, and I didn't care.

I buried my face in the point of her neck where feathers blended with fur. She chirped and started kneading me with her claws. It hurt. I was thrilled.

"I'm sorry you died," I whispered. "I never wanted you to get hurt."

Tempest wriggled from my grasp and nipped me on the nose with her beak. That was enough to break me from my all-encompassing joy. I remembered that she *had* died, that I was in the middle of a test meant for heroes, and my friends had been kidnapped. I scrambled to my feet.

"This is part of the test, isn't it?" I asked, my stomach sinking. Tempest let out a screech, rustled her wings, then proceeded to fly towards the wall behind me. At full speed. She glowed brighter for a moment and passed through the stone as if it weren't even there. She reappeared, winging casually about, darting between tree trunks or passing through them indiscriminately. Then, she landed on my shoulder, as solid as when she had first come into my life.

"You're a ghost!" I was a bit slow on the uptake, but it seemed obvious, now. Why else would she be here? Why else, for that matter, would she be glowing blue?

In all my time working for Death, running his errands, dealing with situations that were both problematic and dangerous, and doing all his marketing, I'd never actually come across a ghost. I'd never met one, I'd never heard of anyone talking about them, nothing. Frankly, I'd assumed that they were the one supernatural or paranormal or whatever thing that didn't actually exist.

Turns out, I was wrong.

Thank the stars for that.

"If you're a ghost, then you can help me," I said. Tempest chirped and ducked her head in a nod. "Can you lead me to where they're keeping Agravane and Neja?"

Tempest huffed and preened her chest fluff, and for a moment, I thought she really was part of this test and wouldn't help me. Then, she flapped her wings and circled my head, trumpeting joyously. A second later and she was flying through the trees at a rapid pace. It took me a second to realise that she wanted me to follow her. I started running.

If you've ever run through a forest, you know that regardless of how cultivated it appears, there are always things to trip over. I wasn't spectacular at running even on flat surfaces, so trying to keep up a steady pace while not tripping over tree roots or sticks or dead leaves was really difficult.

That is to say, I tripped. A lot.

Every time I did, Tempest would fly back to me, squawk or chirp or nip my ear and then fly onwards, passing through trees without flinching. I, on the other hand, had to go around the trees. It was a slow process.

It didn't help that the forest seemed to stretch endlessly in every direction. I knew that this was still in the Goblin Market's pocket dimension, given the ceiling and the slight echo of stone, but the lights were deceptive and disorienting. It was like twilight in any part of the world, and I half-expected to run into birds or foxes or badgers at any moment. The forest, though, was eerie and still, the only noise being my clumsy attempts at trying to run and Tempest's various noises. It could have been that I was scaring off all the wildlife, but I had a feeling there was something else going on here. Something far more sinister.

I hoped Neja and Agravane were alright. If they were not…I shivered, and Sebastian snarled in agreement. We would tear this forest apart, no matter what stood in our path.

After what felt like forever, but was really probably closer to ten minutes of running, Tempest stopped, perching on a low tree branch, her stumpy tail hanging down with the tip twitching slightly. She hissed at what lay before us, and looked at me meaningfully. I rested my hands on my knees, doing my best not to wheeze. When I caught my breath enough not to fall over, I edged my way closer to the chasm that slashed open the earth before us.

I've never been to the Grand Canyon, and most of the heights that I've dealt with have either been in the form of skyscrapers visited for business meetings, or the mountains of the Great Northern Ridge Tribe. I imagine, though, that the chasm before me rivalled the Grand Canyon in size. It was desperately dark, with none of the strange light of the forest spilling into the shadows that clung to the walls. The other side was almost out of sight, though I could barely make out a few treetops swaying in some mysterious breeze. It was not something I could leap over, nor did I see stairs or a bridge or anything of the sort.

It was a test, surely. I imagined that the heros who had faced this particular test had done spectacular things like use magic or build a bridge or a hang glider or something equally impressive. I, on the other hand, had neither the time, patience, or inclination to be impressive. I wanted Agravane and Neja back *now*.

So I stepped up to the edge, leaned over enough that whatever was lurking down there could see my face—because *of course* something was lurking down there—and gave a wave. "Hello!" I called.

Silence.

But not an empty silence. The sort of silence that just screams with startled curiosity. It's the silence that you get in the middle of a crowded room after saying something about having a fondness for dinosaur socks imported from Brazil: people look at you, dying to ask questions but too polite to do so. So they wait. Silent.

This was like that.

Tempest let out a screech of horror and flew to my shoulder. She scolded me, going so far as to nip on my ear. It hurt, but not as much as it had when she was alive, which only made me sad. I shoved the feeling aside and tried again. "Is there anyone there?" I shouted into the abyss. "Because if there is, I'd love to have a chat."

The abyss shifted. It was barely noticeable, but the shadows moved and whatever was down there now fixed its full attention on me. I waited. One beat. Two. Three. Then, the shadows moved some more. Enough that I could see they were not shadows at all, but scales. These were not the neat, dangerous scales of dragons, but more haphazard, some clustered so closely together that light could not escape them, others spaced far enough apart to reveal the leathery skin beneath, it just a shade or two lighter than the darkness.

The scales became a limb, the limb became a leg, the leg eventually revealed the full creature. It was, in a word, massive. Big enough to sleep on the bottom of the chasm with little room to spare. The general shape was difficult to make out given the darkness, but the outline reminded me of a cross between an old Godzilla movie and a sea serpent. A leviathan. It lifted its head until its eyes were roughly level with me and I gulped. There were six of them, three on each side, each glowing bright orange and shimmering with menace and curiosity. And each and every one was focused on me.

I waved again, my mouth dry. "Hi there. I'm Cal Thorpe. I don't suppose you've heard of me, given that this place doesn't seem to require much marketing. I mean, everyone already knows to stay away unless willing to risk their life, correct?"

The creature blinked slowly. I wasn't sure if that was an affirmative or a "get on with it." I kept going.

"Anyways, I'm Death's marketing agent. I do occasional odd jobs for Life, too, though that was really more of an accident than anything. I apologise for the inconvenience, but I'm on a quest."

The leviathan snorted, streams of hot air filling the air like geysers. I pulled off my glasses and cleaned off the fog.

"Yes, yes, I know. A quest. You probably get loads of heros on quests coming through here and could not possibly care less about their search for whatever sacred artefact or cure for the common cold or what have you. I get it. I didn't really want to be on this quest to begin with, but apparently if I do not, then I'll die, and I really, really do not want to die. Does that make sense?"

I was starting to ramble. Tempest stretched her wings, hitting me in the face with her feathers. I spit them out.

"Yes, sorry," I said. "Don't mean to monologue. I was just hoping that I might be able to ask for your assistance in getting to the other side?"

The creature huffed again, this time the hot air missing my glasses. It started to lower itself back down into the chasm, completely unimpressed with me. I cursed silently in every language I knew. Which wasn't a lot, frankly.

"Please?" I asked. "It would really help me out. And I could see about repaying the favour."

The creature halted. Lifted its head and fixed those eyes on me again. They narrowed. Tempest hunched her shoulders, muttering rude noises into my ear. I tried to hush her, but it didn't work.

"You can pay?" the leviathan asked, and I nearly fell into the chasm from the force of its voice. It was earth-shaking, the bass notes ripping through my head. I was fairly certain that my nose was going to start bleeding any moment now.

"What do you want?" I asked. "Let me know and I'll do my best to get it to you."

The creature tilted its massive head, making the world seem lopsided. I swallowed, smoothing the front of my jacket. After an agonising minute, the creature stretched farther up, its arms appearing over the edge of the chasm. I scrambled backwards as it rested them on the ground, squishing a couple of trees as it did so.

"I want stories," it said. "It is so *boring* here. I sleep and I eat and I wait for stupid heros to come and try to cross my den. They are very stupid, making tiny bridges or trying to climb down the side of the wall. It is never a challenge, no work for me. I want entertainment. You can tell stories?"

Those orange eyes narrowed again, as if questioning my ability. I, on the other hand, straightened my shoulders and grinned.

"As it happens, I know a way you can get stories not just from me, but from some of the most interesting creators out there." There would be some logistical issues, of course, like how to get a screen large enough for this leviathan to watch comfortably, and forget about navigating on a phone or with a mouse. But I was going to introduce this thing to streaming services and the internet. And it was going to be fantastic.

For the next half-an-hour, I explained the internet, even going so far as to pull out my phone and show off the social media sites I worked with primarily. Surprisingly, I had great signal here. Then I described television shows and modern streaming services. Once that was explained, with the creature peering over my shoulder at the very tiny phone screen, its breath hot and muggy on my neck, I pulled up the favourite soap opera of Yolanda and Agravane and watched the first episode with the creature.

Tempest chimed in at appropriate times with squeaks and whistles of intrigue and indignation, depending on the characters. I even heard a few earth-rumbling gasps from the creature every now and again. Once the credits rolled, I shoved my phone back into my pocket.

"I can see about getting a projector and screen delivered, so you won't have to worry about the tiny screen," I said. "And there has to be some sort of dictation software that will do the voice commands for everything. I'll figure it out. Once, of course, I get back from my quest. Which means I need to get to the other side so I can find my friends."

I peered at the creature over the rims of my glasses. It was still sniffling, dabbing at its eyes with an enormous clawed finger, mopping up tears. There was a reason why this soap opera was a favourite. Yolanda swore that anyone who didn't cry was heartless. Granted, I hadn't cried, but I was currently missing my soul and emotions were complicated. Yolanda gave me a pass. Barely.

"You will promise me this?" the creature asked. I nodded.

"I will promise."

The creature extended its claw—twice my size in every direction at least—and I took the very tip with both my hands. We shook on it.

I felt a rush of magic binding me to the promise I had made, and I shivered. There was a great deal more to do, I imagined, and I had already made several promises I would have to keep. They were relatively straightforward, but they were still weighty enough to make me feel them. The Goblin Market was dangerous, I knew, but I felt it even more than I had before.

This place could offer you the deepest desires you had and sell them to you for a price you would desperately try to pay. It would strip any person bare in a very short amount of time. Including me.

As soon as the shake was over and the magic bound us, the leviathan reached out and grabbed me. I squeaked as the air was forced out of my lungs, then nearly vomited as I was carried unceremoniously across the chasm and placed on the other side, like riding a really, really bad rollercoaster.

I wobbled on my feet for a moment before leaning against the trunk of a tree. Tempest flew from the other side of the canyon, screeching her annoyance. She landed on my head and buffeted my face with her wings. I patted her weakly, head still spinning.

The creature, our bargain struck, did not bother sticking around to see if I made it in one piece, merely sank back into the shadows of the abyss and disappeared from view. Waiting, I knew, for stories to keep it company. Waiting for me.

I staggered to my feet and started through the forest again, wobbling as I went.

Cheater, the whispers said, echoing through the air like vipers.

"I used my skills," I countered. "You never specified I had to use my physical prowess."

Sneak. Thief. Asking the Darkness for help. They were angry, I could tell. I didn't care.

"I've done far worse things," I said, "and I would do them again. Return my friends to me or see what else I will do to you."

Cheater! The whispers were furious, their speakers almost tangible, almost solid enough that I could tell they were swimming through the air around me. They drew closer.

Sebastian, awake for the first time since entering the forest, lifted its head. I could feel the Reaper abilities taking effect, dimming the colours of the world so that there was only the grey and the yellow auras that told me how long it would be until someone died. The trees were all bright, vibrant, full of life. The air around me, through which the whispers slid, pulsed orange with tiny flecks of silver. These things were longlived, then, but not immortal. Not anymore.

At the sight of Sebastian, or whatever it looked like when it emerged in my human body, the whispers let out screeches that echoed off the rocks and through the trees. They vanished a moment later, leaving the air empty of signs of life.

Tempest perched on a branch above my head, the same transparent blue that she was when I wasn't drawing on my Reaper abilities. I'd never seen the colour of something after death, only before. It stung, still, seeing her like that. I rubbed my chest and shook my head. Sebastian snorted in agreement then went back to sleep. My vision returned to normal and the power in my limbs faded until I was just me.

I started walking again. Nothing else mattered just then except finding Agravane and Neja. I gripped the straps of the rucksack and moved through the trees, Tempest winging her way in front of me.

Then, something happened.

The sound of a heartbeat surged from the bag, loud enough to shake the leaves on the trees.

I gulped. This, as with everything that seemed to be happening on this quest, was not good. Not good at all.

CHAPTER 6

*E*ver since Death lost my soul, my emotions have been haywire. I've vacillated between being more or less emotionless and more or less an emotional mess. I tend to be emotionless much more than I am emotional, which made for very interesting communication skills. Every now and again, one really strong feeling slips through and determines my actions for the next while. In this instance, that determining emotion was fear.

Death's heart beat louder and the trees seemed to close in on me. Tempest kept flying from tree to tree, occasionally turning back and chirping at me as if to ask why I was being so slow. I, on the other hand, was clutching the straps of the rucksack in both hands so tightly that my knuckles were turning white. Sebastian was wide awake and peering around with me, our combined attention taking in every detail of the surrounding area in the hopes that we would see whatever predator would surely be approaching any second, now.

We didn't see it, as it turns out. Sebastian was the first to respond to the danger, and I ducked a moment later. It was too late: a sharp, burning pain flared in my left shoulder. The force of the strike was enough to have me falling to the ground. The strap of my sack snapped and my bag rolled to one side, Death's heart with it.

I reached back and pulled out whatever weapon had struck me in my shoulder, coming up with something that looked like a cross between a bee's stinger and a stiletto knife. Big, dark, and dripping with some sort of poison. It *hurt*. Then, whatever poison was in the dart took effect and my vision flared white while I died and regenerated.

By the time I could see again, only a few moments had passed. It was enough, though, for a massive creature with the body of a reddish lion, a tail pronged with spikes and a head that looked suspiciously human, to pounce on my bag. I'm fairly certain it was a manticore. And it was going after Death's heart.

That, as one might guess, was bad.

"Oh, no you don't!" I shouted and launched myself at the manticore, heedless of the sharp tail, the sharp claws, and, as it turns out, the three rows of sharp teeth that were now turned towards me. It wrapped its jaws around my arm and started shaking me. My glasses flew in one direction and the rest of me flew in another.

When I landed, Tempest leaped in front of me and

screeched at the manticore, her blue form puffed up to twice her normal size. The man-eater grinned, taking a step forward. It had my bag snagged on one paw.

"Run away, little ghost, before I eat you, too," the thing purred, its voice somehow human and feline at the same time.

Tempest just screeched and leaped for the manticore.

I got there first.

Sebastian surged to the forefront of my mind faster than Tempest could fly. It took over, my vision going black and white except for the yellows of the life force around living beings. Shadows formed claws around my hands and I could feel the massive, terrible coils of the monster that was my Reaper form just waiting for me to summon them.

I'd manifested fully as a Reaper the last time someone dared to strike at Tempest. This time, I had barely enough control to stay in a bipedal form. Darkness pooled at my feet. My blood burned in my veins.

"Don't. Touch. Her," I snarled, my voice holding back my wrath by a very narrow margin.

The manticore, to my fury, only smiled wider. "Ah, *now* we have some valuable prey to these forests."

Tempest croaked and hissed, circling around my head on translucent wings. I ignored her.

"Drop the bag and leave," I ordered. "Now."

The manticore looked at the bag on its paw and gave a wicked laugh. "This old thing? It smells enticing, certainly, but not *nearly* so much as you. I can taste your blood on my tongue, Reaper, and there is such power in your veins. Power I could take for my own."

"You're welcome to try," I said, "but it won't work."

The manticore tossed the bag away and crouched low, its claws digging into the earth. Tempest, smart girl that she was, flew after the rucksack and caught it in her claws. She was much smaller than the bag, but managed to carry it to a tree branch over our heads. I turned my attention back to the creature now prowling towards me. It had no idea what was in the bag, which was good, but it thought that I was going to give it the power it wanted, which was bad.

Its poison hadn't done much to me except to trigger one of my regeneration cycles, but I could still feel the place on my arm where its teeth had torn into me. The wound throbbed and my blood, shadowed and fiery, dripped to the forest floor. The ground sizzled where it fell. I would have to die again in order for the wound to be healed, and I hated doing that. A lot.

The fear that had gripped me a few minutes before was now replaced by something much, much more potent. Anger.

I liked to think of myself as a decent person, more prone to long-winded discussions than acts of brutality or violence. I preferred to deal with conflict by finding a logical solution to the problem, just ignoring it, or fighting with sarcasm and snark. I had lost my temper only a very, very few times in my life and all of these instances had been stopped by my friends holding me back. Literally.

Here, though, in this ridiculous forest, being tested

by beings that refused to show themselves and resorted to kidnapping and violence, I had no friends but Tempest nearby. And she wisely stayed out of my way.

So, when the manticore leaped through the air, intent on devouring me for all the power in my body, I lost my temper. Dramatically.

My uninjured arm became shadow itself. I punched it forwards, pushing through the chest of the manticore. The creature let out a horrid cry, clawing at my arm and face, writhing as it tried to escape my clutches. I could feel how this thing might overpower someone; it was strong and swift, a dangerous combination. But right then, my Reaper abilities were more in control than the logical part of me, and I didn't care how strong the thing was. I just held my hand in its chest, slowly letting the shadows melt away until I physically displaced organs and flesh.

Then, I pulled my hand away.

The manticore let out a scream of agony and fell to the forest floor in a heap. It stared up at me, wide-eyed, panting as it bled out before me.

I should have been horrified at what I was doing. I'd never intentionally killed something like this, in anger and blood. All the things that had died at my hand had been accidents or self-defence. I should have been emptying my stomach as the realisation of what I'd done settled on my mind. I should have been. But I wasn't.

I knelt down and picked up my glasses, wiping them clean on my shirt before replacing them on my face. "Ah," I said, looking down at the manticore, "now I can see you."

"You…what…how…" it panted, the yellow aura of its life fading before my very eyes.

I tilted my head and let out a quiet hum. "You really shouldn't go seeking after things that do not belong to you. My power is not one that you can devour."

The manticore let out a whimper, eyes wheeling as it tried to seek on some way to save itself. I heard the whispers floating through the air, their words agitated but too hushed for me to make out. I crouched down next to the manticore, and for the first time, I felt a bit of shame slide into my stomach. It was easy enough to push aside.

"This forest," the manticore breathed, "it's for heroes."

Heroes would not have slaughtered this creature. At most, they would have fought it until it limped away. I wondered how many times this beast had played that game, devouring those who were unworthy and fleeing those who were. No wonder it had no idea what to do with me.

"I'm not a hero," I said as the light slipped away from the manticore's eyes. "I never pretended to be."

The whispers let out a sharp gasp, then fell silent. I rose and wiped some of the blood on my trousers. My arm was still mangled, and would stay that way until I healed or someone killed me, whichever came first. It hurt, but it was a hurt I would hold on to. Like the death of the bartender and guardian, this was something I would remember.

My shadows slipped back into my skin, Sebastian retreating until my vision returned to normal. Tempest gave a questioning screech and fluttered down from the tree, holding the torn rucksack in her talons. She extended the bag to me and flinched away when I took it from her.

"I'm not going to hurt you, my girl," I said, reaching my fingers out. She chirped and hopped forwards, then backwards, finally rubbing her ghostly head on my hands. Her hesitancy stung, though I understood the reason for it. But after a moment, she flew into the air and landed on my shoulder. I scratched her ear and smiled a little as she purred.

I tied the straps of the bag together as best I could before unzipping it slightly so I could check on the jar holding Death's heart. It was unharmed, thank goodness, though it seemed to beat louder by the moment.

"That is a dangerous object to be carrying around so casually."

I yelped, whirled, fell backwards and landed hard on the ground. A bad habit, that. A woman, if you could call her that, peered down at me. She was stunning, beautiful in a way that I couldn't quite describe, and terrifying all the same. Her skin was patterned like a nebula full of stars and her hair floated gently around her shoulders like storm clouds. She wore a dress that shifted colours with her movements. Her feet were bare and left patterns of light where she stepped. But her eyes, they were wide and empty of anything, light, colour, substance. They were voids that would swallow you whole if you looked too closely, and I had seen their like before.

In Death.

"You...You're..." I stammered, stuck between trying to scramble to my feet and cowering away in terror.

The woman—Fate, or whatever name she went by—circled the body of the manticore slowly, clicking her tongue as she went. "Did you have to kill it? There are so few of them left."

"It attacked me," I defended.

"You cannot die," she retorted, flicking a piece of hair over her shoulder, where it crackled with lightning. "The manticore would have killed you once, perhaps twice more, before giving up. You did not need to end its existence."

"It threatened Tempest," I murmured. Tempest had wisely flown away when I fell, but now, she fluttered over to me and rubbed her head on my arm again. "I lost her once."

"A ghost," Fate said, leaning down to peer at Tempest. My miniature griffin hissed, fur puffing out. "Do not be foolish, tiny speck. You are of no interest to me."

I sagged a little in relief. Then, she turned and fixed those voids that were her eyes on me and my relief vanished. Sebastian lifted its head and let out a low, rumbling growl.

"You, on the other hand," Fate said, reaching out to brush her fingers across my cheek. "Are of *great* interest to me."

I wasn't entirely sure what to say to that. Maybe

this meant she would help me find my soul. But then there was the fact that Neja and Agravane were still missing. Not to mention that Fate was Death's *mother* and I had no doubt that grabbing her interest was a really, really bad thing. So I said the first thing that popped into my mind. "Um. Yay?"

Fate chuckled, and at the sound the trees around us seemed to inch—literally—away from her. She clicked her tongue again. "Oh, for goodness' sake! It was *one* time!" She turned to me. "I accidentally laughed hard enough to set a forest on fire. The trees have never forgiven me."

"I see," I said. This was definitely not a good thing.

"Stand up, Calvin Montgomery Thorpe," Fate said. Without even attempting to move my limbs, I was suddenly standing, every part of my body screaming in pain I didn't even know I could feel. Fate stepped around me like she was taking my measurements and I was suddenly very, very uncomfortable. "Humans are such strange things," she said at last.

"Uh, thank you?" I said. Fate stopped before me, the hem of her dress pooled in the manticore's blood. She didn't even seem to notice. I had the sudden urge to run very, very fast. Instead, I stayed as still as possible.

"Relatively fragile, with skin that breaks under less than a pound of force. Your bodies are inefficient for many things, and yet, somehow, you have managed to conquer your realm and are well on your way to conquering Elsewhere. You are prey to many beings, and yet not even dragons are foolish enough to face you head on. A mass of contradictions wrapped up in one tiny collection of nerves and flesh."

Fate grinned, showing off her teeth, which were thankfully perfectly normal. "I like you."

I was beginning to think that Death's mother was insane. It would explain a lot, frankly.

"Thank you?" I squeaked. "Look, I imagine you're rather busy and what-not, but I actually came to find you about—"

Fate waved a dismissive hand. "Yes, yes, you want to find your soul. My son and his ridiculous wife could not manage to do so. So you came to me. An easy enough solution."

That was good, right? Somehow, I didn't quite trust what she was saying.

"And my friends? Agravane and Neja?" I asked. Maybe she was in a good mood and I could be reunited with my soul and my friends before lunch. I doubted it, though.

Fate grinned at me again, this time with a predator's smile. "Oh, foolish man. You thought it would be that easy? You thought you could seek me out and that I would merely wave my hand and let you get on with things? Do you not know who I am? What I am?"

I swallowed. "Death said you were…Fate?"

She laughed. Her hair crackled with lightning again, and I began to feel the hairs on my arm stand up. Sebastian hissed a warning to me and I felt Tempest pressing close to my leg, trembling.

"Fate? It is certainly one means of describing me," she said, trailing a finger over her lips. She lifted her chin and stepped closer. "But it is such an inadequate word. I, who am responsible for the weavings of Time, for the presence of Death, for the tapestry of the world. I am a Weaver and I am a Destroyer. I am beginning and I am end, just as I am ageless and endless. You could hardly expect to understand."

"No," I said in my best placating voice. "I don't understand. But, as you said, I'm just a foolish man. Does that make me any less worthy of your help?"

Fate leaned closer still and whispered in my ear, her breath like velvet on my skin. I shivered. "Who said I cared about *worthiness*? No, little human. I will help you, but not because I care about your worth relative to anyone else's. I will help you because you are going to do something for me."

I gulped. Nodded. What choice did I have?

"Good," Fate said. In a blur of motion, she stepped back and clapped her hands together. The forest fell away in a shiver and we appeared instead in a place that was flat, dry, and almost entirely empty.

"Where are we? Is this where Agravane and Neja are?" I looked around and came up with only grass and scrub and dirt.

"Here? This is Nowhere." Fate smiled.

Then, in a blur of motion, she reached out and touched me on the forehead. Pain blinded me and surged through my limbs, like it was tearing something essential from me and destroying me in the process. I, like any rational person would under these circumstances, blacked out.

CHAPTER 7

"*S*top fretting, he's coming around." Fate's voice was too close for comfort, given that I was still feeling twitchy from pain. I squeezed my eyes closed and willed myself back into unconsciousness. It didn't work.

"No thanks to you," a second voice said. One that was weirdly familiar. Strangely familiar. Bizarrely—

I snapped my eyes open and looked around. I spotted the owner of the second voice and my throat tightened up. I sat up far sooner than was safe and my vision wobbled as a result. When it cleared, I was still not hallucinating. At least, I didn't *think* I was hallucinating. It hadn't happened before, to my knowledge, and frankly I wasn't this imaginative, which usually meant that what I was looking at was actually and truly happening.

"Yes, I'm real. Now take a breath before you pass out again."

The person speaking? It was me. Myself. A mirror

image. Same clothes, though his—mine?—were cleaner than the ones I wore. Everything about us was the same, from the hair to the colour of our skin, to the shoes we wore. Everything, that is, except the eyes. For one, he wasn't wearing glasses. But also, they were entirely black with a bright yellow pupil.

"S-sebastian?" I asked. Myself nodded, expression grim. I was fairly certain I was going to pass out again and started taking deep breaths. After a moment, I managed—barely—to shove the absolute confusion and shock aside, replacing the emotions with as much calm as I could muster. Which, to be fair, wasn't a massive amount.

Tempest popped up just then, floating *through* the ground as if it weren't even there. She was more translucent in the bright sun than she had been in the forest, but I could still see the outlines of her feathers in bright blue. She purred and rubbed her face on my knee, then bounded over and sat happily in Sebastian's lap. I blinked slowly a few times, rubbed my eyes, even took a moment to clean my glasses. Despite all of this, and my hard-won calm, Sebastian didn't vanish.

"You are fine." Fate appeared over Sebastian's shoulder, brow furrowed. Her hair crackled with energy and her expression was very nearly gleeful. "Stop, ah, what's the word…panicking. Yes, stop panicking."

"I'm not panicking," Sebastian and I snapped at the same time. We exchanged a glance, scowled, and turned our collective attention back to Fate.

"If I were panicking," I said, replacing my glasses with care, "I would very likely be screaming. It's an annoying reaction, I'll grant you that, but instinctual. No, I am merely…"

"Frustrated?" Sebastian offered with a tilt of his head that was reminiscent of the being that had taken residence inside me, that terrible manifestation of my Reaper abilities.

"Confused," I amended. "Also frustrated, yes. Mostly confused. Does this mean I'm not a Reaper any longer?"

Fate laughed, tossing her head back. As she did so, the ground quaked and I could have sworn that a few bushes leaned as far away from her as possible. She glared at the offending plant-life. It froze.

"Hardly, Cal Thorpe," she said, folding her arms and staring down the plants. "As if you could be something other than what you are. You are still a Reaper. It is not something that can be taken away, even if I have put your abilities into a separate form. The two of you are still one entity. Just as your soul is still a part of you, despite being separated from you by my son. It happens more than you think, this separation of self. It's not something that you mortals are very good at comprehending, if I'm honest."

I didn't understand at all. I didn't understand the physics—or magic—behind it, nor did I understand the why behind her decision to split Sebastian and I into two. I doubt she did it because she was bored. Or, perhaps not merely bored. There was always an ulterior motive with beings like her. I wanted very much to know what that motive was. But I decided that discretion was the better part of valour and said nothing.

Sebastian, after giving me a look with brows raised, must have agreed, because he stayed silent, too.

"So," I said, changing the subject. "Where are we?"

"Nowhere, I told you," Fate said with a chuckle.

"Let me rephrase: why are we in Nowhere? Wherever that is," I asked. Sebastian pointed to something behind me and I turned, looking at a sign on the side of the road that read, quite clearly:

WELCOME TO NOWHERE, *Oklahoma, Home of the Oldest Tea Shop in the West. Population 102*

"OKLAHOMA." I blinked, looking around at the scrubland, the dry flatness that was the plains. "Do you know, that doesn't make any more sense to me than it did before. Why are we in Oklahoma?"

Fate smirked and lifted her chin. "We're here to find your soul, of course. That *is* why you were looking for me, is it not?"

I leaned closer to Sebastian. "Does this feel a little too easy to you?"

"Indeed it does," he grumbled, eyeing Fate warily. His yellow pupils dilated and I could have sworn I felt the phantom rumbling of those massive, terrible, eldritch coils beneath the surface. I definitely still had a connection to the Reaper part of me. That was enough to make me feel a little better. "We were led to believe that finding Fate would be a difficult challenge. Apart from navigating the Goblin Market, though, losing Agravane and Neja, and that unfortunate run-in with the manticore—"

Tempest let out a hiss and ruffled her feathers.

"The run-in with that creature," Sebastian amended, patting her head, "we did not have to do much at all. She found us."

I touched the strap of the bag that was somehow still on my shoulder. The jar containing Death's heart was there, and the heart was still beating, though it was considerably quieter than it had been in the forest. I looked at Fate as I touched the jar through the bag's fabric. She was busy brushing dirt off her dress and nudging a clump of grass with her toe, cooing to it like a baby. The grass trembled. Fate did not seem to care at all that I was carrying around her son's heart. She had mentioned it the once, but moved on to the manticore almost immediately. Then, essentially without having to ask, she'd brought us here to find my soul?

It was definitely too easy.

"You are quite suspicious, I think," Fate said with a roll of her eyes, turning her attention away from the grass to stare at me. "You must have learned that from Life, because Death certainly does not deserve your suspicion. Can you not just accept that I am here to help?"

"No," Sebastian and I said together.

"Well, that's too bad, because I have no intention of explaining myself. Now, go find your soul, be reunited. I'll deal with you later." Then, without any explanation or assistance at all, not even a wink or nod in the right direction, Fate vanished.

"Do you ever get the feeling that you are a pawn in a game of the universe?" Sebastian asked, holding out a hand to help me to my feet.

"Not really, why?" I asked. "Mostly I just wish people would say what they mean."

"You need to pay better attention," was the helpful response. "Come on, let's go see about this Tea Shop."

"Maybe they serve coffee there, too," I said hopefully. Sebastian groaned and pinched his nose. He shook his head and started walking down the road. Tempest looked at me and I shrugged. She launched herself into the air and settled on my shoulder. Then, the three of us headed into Nowhere.

I'd never been to Oklahoma before, but a part of me had expected a great deal more wheat. Either side of the road, though, was mostly just long grasses and scrubby bushes, with the occasional twisted tree in the way of the sky. There were a few more dots of green in the distance, but not many. It was dry, still, and flat. There was not a single car on the road, which was surprisingly well maintained. If I didn't know better, I'd think that Sebastian and I were the only living things around.

Until, that is, buildings started appearing on the horizon.

For a population of 102, Nowhere was surprisingly organised. There were several houses on the outskirts of town that looked like they belonged to a farm, then the town itself appeared, buildings clustered around the road in neat rows, getting more numerous the closer we drew to a large lake in the distance. There was a single grocery store, pharmacy, home improvement store combined into one, a low brick building with a sign proclaiming it the post office, a couple of other buildings that could have easily been abandoned if it weren't for a car or two out front. Three law offices, for whatever reason. Then, there was the tea shop.

It was an old building, one that had been done in wood and patched with stone over the years to create something that was likely remarkably sturdy but looked like a hodgepodge of bad ideas. There were large pots out front full of colourful flowers, and the windows were wide and bright so that people could both look in and look out. A cheerful place, if a bit of a mess.

Sebastian pulled open the door with a bit more force than was likely necessary. Tempest flew into the building before I could motion to stop her. Not one of the maybe five people seemed to notice, their attention either on their drinks and pastries or on Sebastian and me. I had a feeling that his eyes were going to get us into trouble. Though the gazes were more startled than hostile.

That is, until a woman—young, pretty, red-haired and with a glare that could pierce hearts—stalked up to me and slapped me across the cheek.

"Ow!" I protested, rubbing my jaw. "What was that for?"

"For abandoning me at the depot!" she snipped,

then lifted her chin in the air and sauntered out of the shop with a delicate sniff. I had absolutely no idea what she was talking about.

"Cal," Sebastian growled to me, voice low and deadly. Tempest let out a chirp and perched on a high shelf, her wings spread as if ready to flee at a moment's notice. I, on the other hand, was still nursing my sore jaw and missed the three large, dangerous-looking men who now loomed over me.

They were all of similar features and size, so I guessed they were brothers. They didn't look to be anything other than human, but I was really not very good at telling the difference between human disguises and actual humans. I hoped this was actual humans and not something more bitey, like werewolves. I'd had enough pain for one day.

"Calvin," the one in the middle said, cracking his knuckles. "We need to have a word with you about our sister."

"I beg your pardon?" I asked in my most indignant voice. It usually worked better when I was wearing a well-tailored suit, not the dirty and torn trousers and sweater that was stained with dried blood. Not to mention my wounded arm. I imagined I looked like a mess, not someone to be rightfully indignant. Either way, the man hesitated. He searched my face. Then, he looked at Sebastian and frowned deeper.

"Ah, hell," he said, wrinkling his nose. "Twins. Triplets, I guess, if you're related to who I think you are. Though the accent is new."

The other two men let out various strings of profanity and glared.

"I have no idea what you're talking about. I just want to order a cup of, er, tea, and have a snack. As you can see by the state of my trousers, my morning has not gone to plan and—"

"Shut up," Sebastian said, thwacking me in the arm. "You don't want to bother the gentlemen any more than you already have, *brother*."

I was about to ask why he was calling me brother when we were certainly not that, but Sebastian thwacked me on the arm again, harder, and nodded his head with wide eyes towards the back of the tea shop. Behind the counter, carrying a cardboard box and whistling of all things, was a person who looked very much like me. Another one.

He had my same hair, if a little longer and scruffier, my same face, my same eyes, everything. Except, well, he had a neatly cut beard. And his glasses actually fit. I wasn't sure the beard suited my face, to be honest. It was far less neat than I usually liked. Then again, he was wearing a stained t-shirt and what looked to be shorts beneath a bright pink, frilly apron embroidered with the shop logo on it. I doubted he was terribly concerned with a neat appearance.

He set the box down on the counter and looked up. Then, he froze. His eyes widened, his face went pale, and he let out a string of what sounded like Latin.

"Yeah, you better be scared, Calvin," the man who had confronted me said. "You think that you can get away with not showing up for a date with our sister?

You think you can treat her like that and not face consequences?"

Sebastian stepped up to the man and put a hand on his chest. I felt a ripple of power flutter beneath my skin and knew he was using a tiny drop of Reaper abilities to scare the man. "Sir," he said, voice calm and even a little sharp. "I don't mean to get in the way of your, ah, disagreement with our brother, but we haven't seen him in several years. It would be a shame to have our reunion at a hospital, I think. Perhaps you can sort out your differences another time?"

The man glared at Sebastian, who only looked up at him with those dark, unnatural eyes, and smiled. The man gulped, nodded, and jerked his head to his brothers. They turned and left the shop without once looking back. That left only Sebastian, myself, one old woman with her head bent over the newspaper, Tempest, and *my soul* in the shop.

I walked forwards, my feet gliding over the floor as if it weren't even there. I leaned on the counter. Sebastian stood at my shoulder, hands in his pockets.

"Hello, *Calvin*," I said, a little surprised at the growl in my voice.

"Well...damn. I knew this day would come eventually. I just didn't think there would be two of you. Er, me. How about you have a seat and I'll bring us a pot of tea." Without waiting for an answer, or meeting my gaze, my soul spun around and started fiddling with various tea-making accoutrements, shoulders hunched and muttering to himself in various languages.

"Sebastian," I said in a slow voice. "Why does my soul have an American accent?"

"I have no idea, but the more important thing is that he's now running out the back."

Sure enough, he was making a break for it, the tea entirely abandoned. I sighed.

"I really hate running." Then, with nothing for it but to follow, I set off in pursuit of my wayward soul, Sebastian close on my heels.

CHAPTER 8

"*I* should have worn trainers," I complained, my toes sliding up against the top of my nice leather loafers. I never seemed to be able to pack the right shoes, and the ones I did pack invariably got destroyed. It was a perpetual problem, one I blamed on Life.

"Just run faster," Sebastian snarled. I scowled, but did my best to comply.

My soul, as it turns out, was far better at running than I was. It seemed patently unfair, but there wasn't much to do except continue the chase. It was rather dreary, truth be told. Oklahoma was pretty enough in a dry and open way, but it wasn't my ideal. I much preferred England. Even Scotland would do in a pinch. Running after my soul in such a strange, unfamiliar, empty place was a bit like playing cheerful pop music during a chase scene in an action film. It didn't quite make sense.

Calvin, as I'd mentally dubbed my wayward soul,

given that was what the angry men had called him, was heading directly for the lake on the far side of the tiny town. There weren't any cars there and I didn't see any boats, either, but he must have had an escape route. He had, after all, travelled the long way through history from the early Renaissance to today. I'm sure he'd picked up some useful tips for running away.

I wondered, vaguely, if I would learn those tips once I managed to get him back.

Somehow, I doubted that Fate or Life or whoever was behind this nonsensical situation, would let me have those memories for nothing.

"Cal, stop wool gathering and *run*," Sebastian snapped. He was already several paces ahead of me and gaining on Calvin. I buckled down and pushed through the desire to just stop. Then, I had to push through the desperate wheeze in my chest. And my arm was hurting from the manticore bite. Not to mention my shoes.

What I lacked in physical prowess I made up for in cleverness. Or, well, a desire to end all things running as quickly as possible. I leaned down, picked up a reasonably sized rock, and hoping that I didn't do too much damage, threw it as hard as I could at my fleeing soul. Somehow, I actually managed to hit him.

Calvin yelped and went down, the rock hitting the back of his right knee, though I'd aimed for his shoulder. He faceplanted, hands scrabbling at the asphalt where it turned into a dirt track, legs still churning to right himself. Sebastian slowed to a walk, allowing me time to catch up. I was wheezing and panting and all around a mess. Calvin had scraped the skin from his knees and palms and was glaring up at me with dirt and debris in his beard and hair. Sebastian, curse him, looked perfectly cool and put together.

"I would not suggest running again," he said with a hint of threat in his voice. "We have come a very great distance to find you, and Cal here is very, very bad at running. I would have to do something to intervene if you tried to run again, and I doubt you would like it."

Calvin spat out a glob of spit and dirt, glaring up at us both.

"Why *did* you run?" I managed, finally straightening as I caught my breath. "It's not like I'm here to hurt you."

"Aren't you?" my soul grumbled. "You've been hunting me down like a wounded deer, or don't you think I didn't notice the little spies you've been sending out to try and figure out where I'm at."

I blinked, scratching my head. "I'm just having a really hard time with the American accent. I mean, you used a really terrible double negative in that sentence and I still can't quite figure out what you meant."

Calvin glared harder.

Sebastian crouched down, resting one arm across his knee. I could have sworn that his fingernails sharpened slightly, and the yellow pupils had shrunk to pinpoints. He smiled toothily. It wasn't an encouraging look, and I saw what Yolanda and Agravane meant when they told me not to smile.

"Little soul," Sebastian crooned. "You have been free to run around and do what you like for a very long time, now. But you belong to that man there, and you *must* recombine or we will all die."

"Not me," Calvin scoffed. "I can't die."

"Neither can I," I said. "But we can all fade away until there's nothing left that makes us, us. Or haven't you noticed any of the symptoms?"

Calvin's eyes flashed. He said nothing.

"Headaches," Sebastian offered.

"Tingling fingers," I said, waving my own appendages.

"Emotional flatness," Sebastian continued. "Mental fog. Fatigue. Would you like us to continue?"

Calvin huffed. He sat up and brushed some of the dirt off his shorts, wincing at the bloodstains from where he'd scraped his skin. "Fine. I get it. Did you have to throw a rock at me?"

"Actually, I'm shocked that even worked," I admitted. "I'm terrible at sport."

"We know," Sebastian and Calvin said. They exchanged a glance and glared at each other. To be honest, I felt like glaring, too. Which was strange, given that each of us was really just me.

I was going to need a lot of coffee to sort this one out.

"Why did you run away?" I asked again, this time trying to modulate my tone so it wasn't quite as angry. Judging by the offended look, I don't think I succeeded.

"Like I would want to be paired up with you again," Calvin said with a snort.

"What's wrong with me?" I asked, looking down at myself. "I mean, granted, my clothes are a little tattered, and I could really use a bath and some disinfectant for this arm, but—"

"You're a villain!" Calvin screeched, a little melodramatically for my tastes.

Sebastian pinched his nose. "Stars and stones, he got all your missing emotion, Cal."

I winced. That did sound unfortunate.

Then, I straightened. "Did you just call me a villain? Like, one of the *bad guys*?"

"You are," Calvin confirmed. "I have heard the stories. I know what you've been up to. I can even *feel* what you're feeling sometimes, which is annoying, by the way. Super annoying. As in, I can't even drink my tea unless it's at certain times of day, because you're drinking that idiotic coffee and I can't enjoy coffee flavoured tea."

Sebastian rolled his eyes. "Your inability to enjoy your tea is what has you calling him—us—a villain?"

"I'm not that annoying, am I?" I asked. Sebastian stiffened. Said nothing.

Calvin shuffled to his feet and brushed himself off. He was still a sartorial nightmare, but given the accent, I decided to say nothing. My soul was apparently a complete mystery to me.

"Your being annoying has nothing to do with the fact that you're a villain. A terrible human being, if there's even much humanity left in you." He looked me over and sneered. And if there's one thing that will set a person off, either for good or ill, it's being judged by yourself and being found wanting.

"Is this because I work for Death?" I asked, my voice cold.

"Hardly," Calvin snorted. "I was there when you agreed to work for him in the first place. Remember?"

I ground my teeth. He had a point. Death hadn't lost my soul until I'd accidentally travelled back to 1494, to solve an issue that Time seemed to think only I could fix. "So, what, it's Sebastian?"

Sebastian cast me a dark look, but kept wisely silent. Calvin looked over the Reaper part of me and shuddered, but shook his head.

"No. A Reaper isn't inherently evil. They stand between. Something I've learned during my many, many years of travelling." He lifted his chin. Some dirt crumbled out of the beard he wore. I decided not to point it out. "No, you, Calvin Montgomery Thorpe, are the cause. Do you think I wouldn't hear what you did to trap the dreaming giants? Or that you killed all those souls while Death was on holiday? What about the situation with the rock trolls? You *banished* Eddie without a second thought, leaving him to a crueller fate than being judged by his people."

"It was the logical thing," I said.

"Cal did offer the rock troll a choice," Sebastian chimed in. "We were in accord in that. It is something a Reaper does, or do you not know these things, little soul? You act worldly, but I see little wisdom in your eyes. Or were those men shouting at you regarding treating their sister poorly just an act to throw us off?"

Calvin flushed bright red. He clenched his fists at his side and took a menacing step forwards. I waited to see what move he would make, but I was more than happy to trounce my soul in that moment. In fact, I would have enjoyed it.

"You are cruel. Dispassionate. Listening only to logic, only to some superficial rule of morality that you construct. You think you're so grand, so clever. You work for Death. You're a Reaper. You're above it all." He let out a dry laugh. "And you don't even know, do you? That it's all a lie. That you've bought into the reality spoon fed you by beings who care nothing for us. Or do you honestly think that Fate leading you here was done out of the kindness of her heart?"

I shifted the bag on my back, feeling the jar inside shifting slightly. I tried not to think about the beating heart inside. It was true. Fate hadn't even asked for her son's heart back. She had just ignored it, like it wasn't important or relevant. Like she was there for me, not the heart. And yet Death had been so eager to hand it over. Life, at least, was honest in her interest in me; she knew I didn't like her and enjoyed tormenting me over it.

"Being logical and dispassionate does not make me the villain," I said.

"Doesn't it? Do you even care that your friends Agravane and Neja have been taken from you?" Calvin asked.

Sebastian reached out before either of us could react, his fingers wrapping tightly around Calvin's throat. This time, I definitely saw his nails sharpening, tiny pricks of blood forming at their tips. "How do you know about Agravane and Neja?" the Reaper hissed, fingers darkening into shadow. I could feel his fury beneath my skin, but it was distant, empty. My own curiosity was just as vibrant, though. I stepped closer to Calvin and together Sebastian and I bore down on him, waiting for an answer.

"I am your *soul*," Calvin gasped, scrabbling at Sebastian's arm. He could not penetrate through the writhing shadows. "I know your friends, your enemies, your joys and dreams and terrors. Just because you have no idea what I've been doing these last centuries does not mean I am not intimately aware of your actions. They come like dreams in the night. Though, I usually only remember big things, like your encounter with Eddie."

"Do you know where they are?" Sebastian snarled. "How to get them back?"

"I know *his* thoughts, not those of some ridiculous testing ground!" Calvin snapped, pointing at me. Sebastian released him with a snort of disgust. My soul staggered back, rubbing at his throat. As I watched, the small wounds closed up and vanished. The scrapes on his knees and hands were still there, so why these wounds? Unless...

"We cannot harm each other," I murmured. "Fate won't let us, will she?"

Calvin scoffed. "No, really?" His sarcasm was palpable. "Who do you think got us into this mess to begin with? Do you honestly believe that Baz chasing off a guy with a gun who was guarding the dreaming giants' prison, sending this guy straight on his way to murdering you, was a coincidence? Do you honestly believe that you dying was normal? A mugging at gunpoint, in London? It's absurd!"

Sebastian nodded. "He has a point, Cal."

"Of course he has a point!" I snapped. "I'm not an idiot."

"Then why haven't you figured out what my note meant yet?" Calvin asked. He was referring to the note that Neja had found through her mortal realm contacts, one penned in Croatia some three or four centuries back. It had said, *The employment was a mistake.*

I had never figured out what it meant.

To be honest, I hadn't tried that hard. I liked my job.

"Death didn't mean to hire you, Cal," Calvin said quietly. He almost looked sorry to be telling me this. He flicked his gaze to Sebastian, who let out a long breath, looking just as uncertain as I felt. "He made a mistake. I only learned of it after we were separated. When my memories were unblocked."

"Unblocked," Sebastian said. "Death blocked the memories? Or Fate?"

"Death, I think," Calvin said. He rubbed his head. "It gets a little fuzzy when I try to push it. But I know that he didn't mean to hire you, Cal. It was a mistake. An error."

"But...what about everything that happened afterwards? What about Sebastian?"

"I think you were always meant to be a Reaper," Sebastian said. "It's not something that one can aspire to, it merely is. Just like our mother is a Knight."

Calvin nodded. My head was starting to spin at this

point, and I really needed to get out of the sun and into a nice, comfy chair with the largest cup of coffee ever so I could figure all this out. I took off my glasses and put a hand over my eyes.

"Wait. Just…wait. Let me see if I understand all this correctly. Death wasn't meant to hire me, but he did because of an error. I lost my soul, became a Reaper, various other adventures, and now here I am, with both my Reaper powers and soul manifested before me. Set on this particular path by Fate. Only, my soul thinks I am a villain because I am at odds with my emotions, because I don't care? So he won't cooperate with me. Does that sum things up nicely?"

I may not have had a massive amount of emotional wherewithal, but I was, at that particular moment, very in touch with my anger. And I was angry.

"You utter bastard!" I snarled, lunging for Calvin. He yelped and scrambled backwards, managing to evade my grasp with annoying ease. I lunged again and again until I managed to wrap one fist in his shirt and swung the other at his face. It made a very satisfying *thump* when I clocked him and I was very tempted to do it again, despite my aching fingers.

"What are you doing?" Calvin screeched, dancing back towards Sebastian and rubbing his jaw. "That hurt!"

"It had better hurt, you mooncalf'd turnip," I hissed. "The only reason I am cold and logical instead of caring and whatever else you think I should be, is because *you* got all the emotion! Sure, I can get emotional if I have an overwhelming need to do so—

like now, when I'm considering strangling you—but that's it. I can't feel more than a baseline most of the time. I can't read other people's emotions. I can't feel sad or happy or *anything* unless it's so overwhelming it chokes me! And because of this, because *you took* everything that I feel, you think *I'm* the villain? I could say the same about you!"

I leaped for Calvin again, wanting to get my hands around his throat so I could throttle him. Sebastian intervened, stepping between us.

"Stop, both of you," he hissed.

We stopped, but Calvin stuck his tongue out at me and I stared at him with all the murder in my heart. Sebastian sighed.

"Before the separation of you two, we were never this volatile," he said. Then, he winced. "You know what I mean. Pronouns are hard when you're talking in triplicate."

It might have been that Sebastian had a point. A tiny, itty bitty point. Before Death accidentally lost my soul, I may not have been the equivalent of a chatty Vulcan, as Agravane and Yolanda called me, but I was never effusive, either. That was the result of growing up with my mother, who was as outwardly emotional as a fierce garden statue, though she was a very good person. I was never good with emotional reactions and tended to be far more practical. But now...

I could feel what little practicality I had slipping away as my anger grew. It was difficult to think logically while provoked by the idiot that was my soul. I tried to hold on to a shred of sense. I took three deep breaths, closing my eyes to solidify my focus. It worked. Sort of. I was still furious, but I could push it aside to have a rational conversation.

"I—we—need to recombine, or we're all going to implode," I said. "Or explode, as the case may be. I know you've been on your own all this time, but you *know* that we're meant to be one entity. You're my soul!"

Calvin sniffed. "Do you have any idea what it's been like? I'm a human, Cal, and I just walked through history without being able to grow old or die. I'm immortal. Completely immortal. And I have no magic to endear me to the magical creatures who live here. No human could get close enough to me to know my secret. I've literally live a hundred lives, just to stay safe and away from being experimented on by the government. I've seen both world wars, and countless others. I'm so *tired*, Cal."

I saw it, too, that weariness in his eyes. In my eyes. Was this what I would feel in another five hundred years, when everything I had known had fallen away and Elsewhere and the mortal realms were unrecognisable? Yolanda and Agravane would be gone, neither of them possessed of that particular gene that gave immortality like a gift. But Death and Life would still be there. Baz would still be there. Neja. Others.

I held out my hand. "You're not alone anymore," I said slowly. Calvin shuddered.

"We took this job with Death so we could keep living," I continued. Sebastian nodded, slipping his hands into his pockets as if he were perpetually calm and cool and collected. "So let's keep living."

Calvin shook my hand. "Very well."

"This is all well and good. Only one problem," Sebastian said. "I have no idea how to actually recombine us. Oh, and there appears to be a pickup truck with, how would you say, ya-hoos, leaning out the window and shouting at us."

We all turned to see the truck that was, indeed, bearing down on us. Leaning their heads out the windows were two of the three brothers that had confronted me at the diner. Calvin gulped audibly.

"Any ideas?" I asked, already dreading the answer.

"Run," Calvin said.

Not again.

CHAPTER 9

"What did you do?" I demanded as we ran. Sebastian was ahead of both Calvin and I. Surprisingly, I managed to keep up with my soul quite well. I had a feeling that the large truck bearing down on us was a factor; I was far more motivated by fleeing dangerous situations than running towards something. Yolanda said my fight-or-flight response was over developed in the flight direction.

"It's not my fault!" Calvin insisted. He was limping slightly, likely because I hit him with a rock. I couldn't bring myself to mind. He deserved it. "Their sister wanted to meet me at the depot and I never showed because I'm *not interested*!"

"Yes, I met her," I grumbled. The memory of that slap was quite vivid. The truck revved its engine and the men chasing us let out whoops. We were drawing closer to the water, and the road had turned to gravel marked with divots and holes. Thankfully, it slowed down the vehicle so that us mere humans—

and Sebastian—could outrun the thing. The only problem was that the road was also ending very shortly.

"The lake!" Sebastian called over his shoulder, gesturing to the large body of water. Calvin pointed to the right and my Reaper abilities nodded, ducking off the road and into a copse of trees. A moment later, he vanished. Calvin and I followed.

The ground fell away between the trees, revealing a small path that ran parallel to the water, but was down from the road by about ten feet. It wasn't quite a cliff, but it was close enough. I slid, my wounded arm screaming as I caught it on some roots. I'm fairly certain I left my blood behind, but at least I managed not to drop the rucksack carrying Death's still-beating heart.

Tempest let out a screech and dived towards the lake, her fur flickering with droplets of water as she flew in and out. She seemed perfectly happy, unaware that we were being followed. Granted, she was a ghost, and I doubted that the angry humans could see her, let alone harm her.

Calvin pulled me along the path a little farther, then we ducked into a tiny cave carved out under the overhang. It was barely big enough for the three of us, plus the metal chest that was already stowed there. Sitting on top of the chest was a sword, covered in a tooled leather scabbard, the hilt topped with what looked like an actual ruby.

"What is all this?" I asked.

"Shut up, Cal," Sebastian snapped. I did as I was

told, the sound of footsteps on gravel sounding from not too far away.

"Where did they go?" one of our pursuers asked.

"Probably leaped into the lake. They'll have to come back to town at some point," the other said. There was some shuffling around and then I heard a plop as they threw a rock into the water.

"Come on, no point wasting time here. My shift starts in half an hour. Besides, Louise needs to stop chasing out of towners. It's getting a bit ridiculous."

There was some more grumbling, a few more stones kicked over the overhang, then the telltale sound of footsteps heading in the opposite direction. I heard two doors slam, then the truck engine roared to life and sped off in the opposite direction.

Sebastian shoved against me and I stumbled out of the cave and into the water. "Great," I said, lifting my feet to stare at my shoes. "These were nice shoes!"

"There wasn't enough space for all of us," Sebastian sniffed. Then, he turned to Calvin, who was surreptitiously reaching for the sword. "What is all of this?"

"All of what?" Calvin asked, his voice too high to be honest.

"The sword? The chest? The giant ruby?" I asked.

"Oh, you know, just a few...souvenirs I picked up on my way through history. Just enough to sell if I needed the funds quickly." He brushed his hand over the chest almost fondly and I frowned.

"You would sell this stuff? Surely you'd have done so already, if you were wanting to move quickly. A sword with a ruby the size of an apricot isn't likely to be inconspicuous if you show up in a new town. Not to mention hauling a chest like that is—"

"Cal," Sebastian said, dark eyes glinting. "Shut up."

I shut up. Calvin knelt before the chest, his shoulders hunched. It took me a moment, but I figured it out. "Oh. They're sentimental items."

"How much of my travels will I remember when we're joined together?" Calvin asked, voice hard. He ran a finger over the sword and pulled it into his lap before unsheathing it. The blade was finely honed, shiny, and very likely very old. I wondered if my soul could use it, or if he was as helpless at fighting as I was. "Will I remember the friends I had or the lessons I learned, or will it all be absorbed and forgotten, just like my individuality?"

"Your individuality?" Sebastian asked. There was a slight purr to his tone that made the hair on the back of my neck stand up. I winced and settled on climbing out of the water so I could pull off my socks and lay them in the sun, even if for a few minutes. "Do you not understand, little soul, that we three are all the same?"

"Are we?" Calvin asked. "I've lived five centuries while Cal here got to travel through time in a single leap. It's been what, two years for you since you lost track of me? Which one of us has lived more?"

"You don't know what I've lived through," I said, thinking of the various transgressions I'd made, especially in the name of a good cause. Trapping the dreaming giants and the exousia. Banishing the leader of the rock trolls. The souls I'd accidentally killed while filling in for Death. It didn't matter that they were dying anyways, that the angels and giants were battling to rule the mortal realms, that Eddie had been trying to lead his people to war. I'd done things that weren't exactly…noble. And I'd got away with it.

"Don't I?" Calvin mocked. "I see your life in my dreams?"

"But do you feel his turmoil?" Sebastian asked. "Our turmoil? Even without your emotions, the things we've done—"

"Enough," I said. Both Cal and Sebastian fell silent, watching me. "None of our experiences are less valid than another's. Or do we need to start fighting on the ground again?"

"You started it," Calvin muttered. I shoved aside the flare of anger and my soul stiffened, as if he could feel what I'd done. Perhaps he could.

"Anyways, I don't know how much you'll—I'll—remember. Fate seems to be the one holding all the answers and I have no idea how to find her." If I couldn't find Fate, I would have to make my way back to the Goblin Market on my own and retrace my steps to find Agravane and Neja. I'd probably have to make several more bargains, the binds of which I already felt around my neck.

"What about Death's heart?" Sebastian asked. Calvin fumbled with the latch on the metal chest, the lid crashing down. "Could we find her with that?"

"You're carrying Death's *heart* around?" Calvin hissed, eyes wide. He scratched at his beard and looked around like he expected some dangerous magical creature to launch itself at us from any direction.

"I guess your dreams missed that piece of information," I said, patting my bag. The heart beat strongly inside. I could feel it through the glass and fabric, like a shock after walking on carpet and touching the light switch. I flinched.

"Do you have any idea how dangerous that is?" Calvin asked. He hunched his shoulders, still looking around.

"We are aware," Sebastian said drily. "Now, can we use Death's heart to find Fate or not?"

I shrugged. "I wouldn't even know where to start. I mean, we could carry it around like a beacon, but there's no guarantee that she would come when called. We had to travel to the deepest parts of the Goblin Market to find her in the first place, and that lost us Agravane and Neja. Besides, she didn't even seem to care about the heart when she left us here."

Calvin scratched his beard, expression thoughtful. I wondered if it itched regularly. I hated even the feeling of stubble and shaved often. Having a full beard, no matter how well trimmed, was a nightmare of mine. "What if—and hear me out before you go ignoring me —but what if we just went to find Agravane and Neja instead of looking for Fate?"

Sebastian growled deep in his throat, the sound more animalistic than human. "Being separate is dangerous. The longer we are apart, the more our condition deteriorates."

Calvin snorted. "We're not going to fade away in the next ten minutes, are we? I think we'll be fine."

"Unless one or all of us gets killed and has to

revive," I said. "I don't know how often we have before that takes up too much energy and we all fade away into nothingness."

Calvin glared at me, but even my stubborn soul could not deny that I had a point.

"We may not have much choice," Sebastian admitted. He nodded his head to the bag. "Just because we have such a powerful beacon does not mean that Fate will appear. She obviously only appeared last time because we fit some piece of her plan. She has her own agenda, her own idea of how things should play out. And if she is not immediately putting the three of us back together, we must assume that it does not suit her plans at the moment."

The three of us scowled. I hated being manipulated by supremely powerful beings, and I had no doubt that the other two of me likely hated it as well. Fate was spoken of by Death with a sort of reverence that went beyond the devotion of a son; in fact, I'd bet heavily that he was slightly afraid of her. I didn't know what this whole mistake was with him hiring me, but if Fate had her fingers in any of the pies, it was probably bad. And dangerous.

Neither of which I liked.

I hated being manipulated by people, especially powerful immortal people. They always pushed way too much.

"Alright," I said. I tested my socks to see how dry they were. Some, but not quite enough to be comfortable in wet leather. Another pair of shoes ruined. "Alright. Fine. We need to get our friends back, then we'll see about Fate. We need to get back to the Goblin Market."

"Where, exactly, did you lose them?" Calvin asked. "The information I received was…indistinct. It came just as I was getting up for the day."

"There was some sort of testing ground," I said, waving my hands.

"The resting place of the doomed." Sebastian gave a sniff of disdain. "Some sort of ridiculous place where supposed heroes—"

"The resting place of the doomed?" Calvin asked. "Seriously? I thought that place was defunct. It was out of favour when I went through the Market two centuries ago. Anyone with half a brain can solve the challenges, not just heroes. Why would you go there?"

"Well, there was this guy who said we could find Fate there." Even to my ears, that sounded foolish. "Piffle."

"We have to go back," Sebastian said with a sigh.

"Should I find us a flight to Austin?" I was already pulling out my phone to search for flights out of the nearest airport. I had no idea how we were going to convince the bookstore owner to let us back through without some of those silver coins Neja had paid with, but surely there were other currencies one could pay with.

"No need." Calvin flung the lid of the metal trunk open and started digging through the contents. I spotted a few things like old books, what looked like a Faberge egg, a cowbell, and a whole set of silverware. These were the artefacts he had? What sort of sentimental value could they hold? I had no idea, and I wondered how many of the items would mean something to me after we'd been recombined. His fears now seemed valid.

He pulled out what looked like a silver net from the bottom of the trunk, and three crimson candles. "I never thought I'd actually need this," he said, dusting off the candles, "but I kept it just in case."

We climbed away from the trunk—after he locked it up, of course—and Calvin set the net on the ground, pinning it in place with the candles. The whole thing was barely big enough for a large man, let alone three people.

"Step into the middle," Calvin instructed. He scratched his beard, adjusted his glasses, and joined Sebastian and I on the silver netting. "It's like a summoning circle, but in reverse. The net is charged with magic and the candles were bought from the Market, so they serve as guides. I'll activate it—"

"Get a move on, would you?" Sebastian grumbled. "I would prefer not to be in such close proximity. You both smell."

Calvin muttered something rude under his breath, then took a deep breath. He lifted his hands, which hit both Sebastian and I in the shoulder and face respectively, then started chanting something in a language I'd never heard before, but was some sort of French derivative. A Creole dialect, perhaps? Pidgin French? I didn't know.

I barely had time to contemplate this when the net sprang to life, filling the air with thousands of glowing motes that stung every time they touched my skin. I yelped as one landed on my injured arm, then the world went entirely black. My stomach leaped into my throat and I lost whatever food I had onto my already ruined shoes.

Then, we were in the Goblin Market again.

CHAPTER 10

This part of the Goblin Market was completely new to me. Mostly because we were in a building. Also, the building was moving, the motion wobbly and halting, like someone trying to walk after drinking a few too many pints. For once, the place was not a bar or saloon or any other alcohol dispensing joint.

It was a coffee shop.

My nose was filled with the aromatic flavour of roasting coffee beans, a scent I was particularly fond of. The sound of espresso machines filed the air, over-laying a soft, comfortable jazz album playing in the background. The floors were hardwood, the walls a pleasant, muted green, and there were several tables arranged throughout the room with a few people there, reading or talking or working on laptops.

I don't know how, or why, but we were in a coffee shop in the Goblin Market, and I was perfectly alright with that.

Sebastian, on the other hand, let out a sigh. "Great. We'll lose him for at least an hour."

"We don't have time for coffee!" Calvin insisted, grabbing my arm. His other hand was resting on the giant ruby in the hilt of his sword. I hadn't realised that he had brought it with him, and frankly, seeing myself —even an entirely different version of myself— wearing a sword was ridiculous. Judging by the dark look in his eyes, though, I had no doubt that he believed it necessary.

It was, to be honest, a bit saddening.

Tempest appeared in mid-air a moment later, chattering madly. She buffeted Calvin with her wings, flew in a circle around Sebastian, and finally landed on my shoulder. I reached up to pet her and earned a nip from her beak instead. I suppose it was retribution for not being able to fit the miniature griffin in Calvin's little transportation net.

"Where are we?" I asked, taking in another heady sniff of coffee beans.

"The Hut," Calvin said. He looked displeased. "I tried to aim for a more *stable* landmark, but *apparently* someone else was thinking of coffee."

I had a feeling that someone was me. I had been thinking of coffee—I was always thinking of coffee— specifically the type of coffee that I marketed. I had discovered it in the Market and made a deal with the owner for free coffee for life in exchange for marketing. As far as I was concerned, it was a great deal.

"Cal Thorpe!" a high, clear voice said. I whirled, as did the rest of me, and spotted the very brownie who had sold me the coffee. She was dressed in silk, her wrists stacked with shining jewellery. At her side stalked a large, dog-like creature that looked like both protection and an exotic pet, at least judging by the massive diamond-studded collar it wore. "What are you doing here?"

She dashed forwards, her diminutive form barrelling into me at full force. Despite the luxury, she was exactly as I remembered: short, furry, with the sort of face that you trust. I hugged her back, ignoring my dirty clothes and ruined shoes and the effect they would likely have on her silk. It was nice to see a friendly face.

"Hi, Ophelia," I said. "How are you? Been spending that coffee money, I see."

She waved a hand, her bracelets catching the light. "You tease me. You know full well that I would not be earning so well if you hadn't offered me our deal. Speaking of, can I get you some coffee?"

"We don't have time for this, Cal," Sebastian murmured in my ear. He was glowering, shadows dancing just under the surface. I knew that we had to find Agravane and Neja, but we would never do that without information, and a coffee house was exactly the sort of place one got information.

Ophelia frowned, tiny points of fangs showing on her lip. She studied me, then Sebastian, then Calvin. "Why…are there three of you?"

"It's a long, complicated story," I said. I shoved my glasses up my nose. "I will happily take some coffee. Then we can talk? Perhaps you can help us."

The brownie's frown deepened, her bright eyes narrowing. After a moment, though, she nodded. She raised a hand and snapped at the barista, a haggard looking harpie, then nodded towards a table in the corner. It was roped off and had all the looks of someone's home office. There were papers strewn about, a laptop, a phone, and various pens.

"I work here," Ophelia explained. "I bought the Hut last year. What better place of business than a moving coffee house? Though we've had to make allowances for the motion. No open containers, bolting the furniture down, that sort of thing."

As if on cue, the house lurched and righted itself again, like it had tripped. Perhaps it had, leaving some unfortunate Market-goer now needing medical care. I decided not to ask about any more particulars, instead sitting at the table beside Ophelia. Sebastian and Calvin joined us, the former glowering darkly, the latter grumbling under his breath in several different languages.

The brownie waited until we'd all been served coffee. I took a deep drink, savouring the rich taste, feeling the warmth down my throat. It had been too long since my last cup. That was the problem with quests like these; they rarely allowed for coffee breaks. It wasn't the caffeine, as Yolanda and Agravane both agreed that I was equally grumpy before and after the coffee, no matter the time of day. It was the pure joy of having a warm drink, of having that moment of peace where things were quiet enough that I could enjoy the ritual. That was what I loved.

I took another, smaller sip then set down my cup. I folded my fingers together and looked at Ophelia with frank openness.

She swirled a spoon in her own cup, the milky liquid frothing slightly from the motion. "I've heard some interesting rumours lately."

"Interesting, how?" Sebastian growled, leaning closer in his chair.

The brownie smirked. "Not nearly interesting enough to explain why you now exist in triplicate, dearest Cal."

I felt Death's heart in the bag now resting against my leg and could have sworn that it was beating stronger. I did my best to ignore the potential omen. "Let's just say that there was a mix-up with Fate and my soul and Reaper abilities are now…sentient."

Ophelia's eyes widened with alarm. "Separate, too? That does not bode well."

"It will be remedied shortly," Sebastian snapped.

"Be nice," Calvin chided, though he looked no happier about being there than Sebastian did. "My dear," he said, his American accent particularly strong. I winced, as did Ophelia. "I realise that this may be an imposition, but we require directions."

"Directions?" Ophelia batted her eyes at my soul and I frowned. "I do believe you know the rules of the Market, Cal. Nothing, not even directions, without payment in return."

Calvin sighed. "And, what, I suppose you already know what you want?"

Ophelia laughed, spreading her hands. "What more

could I possibly want? I have a coffee empire, kindly marketed by yourself. No, we need not make a bargain. We're just talking, us four. All I was saying is that I've heard interesting rumours."

"What sort of rumours?" I asked.

"That you angered some of the Elderkin." The brownie leaned forwards, shoving her coffee cup aside with less care than I would have expected. Several drops of coffee splashed over the edge and landed on some of the papers. I noticed that many others had this same effect. I wondered if that was normal for her, or if the strain of having to run a coffee empire was getting to her. My business was to do marketing, not to worry about how her empire was run. I shook myself, forcing my hand to the task at hand.

"The Elderkin?" Sebastian asked. "The last Elderkin we encountered was The Morrigan, and we made it very clear how we felt about her interference."

"Not all Elderkin are as…coherent as The Morrigan," Calvin said. "I've met several who are no more than whispers from forgotten times and shrines. Old gods who haven't fallen into the category of legend or lore. Who have no one to remember them."

Ophelia let out a dramatic sigh, her teeth bared in a vicious smile. "Alas, it is truly a terrible thing to see such powers fall into nothingness."

I raised my brows. "You do not care for the Elderkin?"

"I care for no one who would oppress those of us who are inherently less powerful. You're a Reaper, one of the biggest badies out there, as it were, but us lesser powers know that we can count on you. The Elderkin were almost all universally bullies. I say anger them all you like."

I knew that some in Elsewhere cared more for power than just about anything, but to hear Ophelia's vehemence regarding the practise was concerning. I recalled sitting at a table with a brownie, a selkie and a few other "lesser" powers when I visited with the rock trolls. This was about a week ago, and the glimmers of gratitude for my deigning to notice them still stung. Just because I was a Reaper and they were weaker, my notice was like a gift from above. It was…disheartening and disconcerting at the same time.

"How, exactly, have we angered the Elderkin this time?" Sebastian asked, when it became clear that I was unable to voice my thoughts aloud in any sort of coherent matter. It kept happening, this mental diverging. I couldn't quite focus on the present, focus on trying to find Agravane and Neja. Everything struck me as interesting and so I followed it.

Was this some sort of side effect of being split in three? If so, I didn't like it.

"The rumours aren't very specific, given that most of them came from the place of no questions, but they say that you ventured into the resting place of the doomed and battled your way through the clutches of the Elderkin that rule there." Ophelia chuckled darkly. "I would have loved to see that."

"Wait," Calvin said, holding up a hand. "The resting place of the doomed, it's ruled by Elderkin?"

"Of course! Who else would care about the proving

ground of heroes but old gods? Ones with no one else to defend them, either. I'm surprised they've lived this long, but then, the place is surrounded by myth and mystery. There must be enough reverence to keep them alive." Ophelia took a large sip of coffee and clunked her cup down again. I winced.

My head was starting to ache.

"Then those whispers…" I glanced at Sebastian and he nodded, yellow pupils narrowed into points. I could practically feel the anger radiating off of him.

"Old gods," he said. "Ones with very little to lose."

"We need to get Agravane and Neja back immediately!" Calvin slammed his fist onto the table, making the rest of us jump. He did not look at all apologetic, instead leaning into the emotion that I lacked.

"We *need* directions," I said.

"Directions to where?" Ophelia asked, once again batting her eyes at me. I hesitated. As much as I liked the entrepreneurial brownie, I didn't need this particular information sold around the Market. Not if there were other parties interested in the three of me. Or what I was carrying. As much as I'd like to forget about Death's heart in the bag at my feet, the insistent heartbeat was persistent.

Death had warned me it was a dangerous thing, to walk around with all this power. Before, I hadn't really worried about it, as the heart seemed secure and hidden in the jar and bag. Now, I was worried that those thin layers of glass and fabric would not be enough. Already, the hungry gleam in Ophelia's eye was becoming more intense, though I doubt she was searching for the artefact I carried. No, she was just interested in power, and I had it.

I took a hasty sip of my coffee. "How do we get out of the Hut? Is there some special ladder? Some sort of magic carpet?"

"No, it stops every half hour. I think it's still looking for its old keeper. The witch."

Calvin stopped fidgeting with the sword at his hip. He licked his lips. "What witch?"

"Mmm, I think she went by Baba Yaga in some Russian folklore, but there are several of those. You met one last time, I think, Cal. The Iron Witch?"

Yes, and that interaction had not gone particularly well. She'd spilled my coffee, I'd got into a fight, then discovered I was not entirely human or mortal anymore. This was before I knew that I was a Reaper, before any of it made sense. The Iron Witch had been dangerous, and certainly a near match for me, even in my ignorance. I did not want to meet any more of that particular breed of witches.

"Wait," I said. "Wasn't the Iron Witch Elderkin?"

Ophelia nodded. "I think so. There aren't many witches of that calibre around any more. Some of Baba Yagas claim to be Elderkin, though I think there was only one true Yaga, and she died ages ago. At least, her heart was ripped out and turned to stone."

Calvin's hand covered the ruby on his sword. I had a sinking feeling in my stomach. Then, before I could say anything to my soul, regarding his sword or witches or just where the exit was, the Hut shook itself vigorously, spilling drinks and papers and patrons all across the floor.

It fell still a moment later, the lights flickering.

"I can feel it in there," a voice cackled, deep and aged and malevolent. "The beating of a heart. It wouldn't happen to be mine, would it, *dushenka*?"

I looked at Calvin. Sebastian looked at Calvin. Everyone else in the place, thankfully or not, cowered and panicked, ignoring the three of us completely.

"What did you do?" I asked my soul. He didn't meet my gaze, his hand tightening reflexively on the hilt of the sword.

"Should we run?" Sebastian asked drily.

"We'd never be able to outrun her," Calvin said. He stood and drew his sword in a fluid motion I knew I'd never be able to replicate. "No, we stay and fight."

Suddenly, I had a great dislike for my soul. Greater dislike for my soul, that is, since we weren't getting on terribly well to begin with.

CHAPTER 11

The Hut rattled again, like a bird shaking out its plumage. The voice cackled from outside, and I could have sworn that it was louder. A moment later and windows that had been papered over to match the rest of the walls and block out the view of the Market burst inwards, glass flying everywhere.

"It's been far too long," the witch crooned, her voice flowing through the windows with dangerous intent. "I've been waiting for you, *dushenka*."

"Well, come and get me," Calvin roared, brandishing his sword.

"Cal, hold on to that heart," Sebastian murmured, shoving my bag into my hands. "And keep out of the way. I have a feeling that our soul has caused far more trouble over the years than he let on."

"Gee, what gave you that impression?" I grumbled, but did as I was asked. In fights, it was an unfortunate truth that I was fairly useless. Agravane had taught me how to throw a decent punch, but I broke my finger twice before getting it right. Barely. I was, however, exceptional at ducking.

In this case, I ducked behind the overturned table with Ophelia. "Sorry about your coffee shop," I muttered. "Apparently my soul neglected to tell me a few salient points about his activities over the last few centuries."

The brownie stared at me with wide eyes, her hands clutching at some papers that were now completely covered in spilled coffee. "What is going on, Cal?" she demanded.

"Once I find out, I'll let you know."

There was a crash, then the door—which was apparently hidden behind a potted fern—flew inwards, scraping across the floor. Silhouetted in the doorway was the figure of a short, stout woman with hunched shoulders, rounded back, beaked nose and bent knees. She stepped into the cafe and her features came into sharp relief. Her skin was greying and wrinkled, her clothes worn, bloodstained and ripped. Her hair was white, bound up in a scarf of faded red. Her eyes were the only thing that looked young, showing a bright, vivid blue that was far more intelligent than I would have liked. Worst of all, her teeth were made of iron, flecked with rust. They clacked together as she surveyed the room.

She froze, tilting her head to one side like a bird. "My, my, isn't this a surprise? There are two of you!"

I assumed she was talking about Calvin and Sebastian, given that I was ducked behind a table. I inched my head backwards so she wouldn't see me watching the events.

"Here," Ophelia murmured, holding out her phone. It was set to the camera and with the lens peeking out from behind the table, we were able to watch everything that was going on. The situation was not encouraging, even with the reduction in detail on the small screen.

Calvin was standing at the ready with his sword. He looked, if you disregarded the shorts and stained t-shirt, fierce. I think it was the beard. Sebastian, though, radiated calm and collection. His hands were in his pockets, his posture was relaxed, his expression bored.

"I beat you once, witch," Calvin said in the sort of tone one used for grand speeches in theatre. This was definitely the wrong setting for that sort of tone. My soul had a death wish. "I'll do it again."

"I would like to see you try, *dushenka*."

"What does that mean?" Sebastian asked casually. "I'm not familiar with Russian."

"It means little soul," Calvin ground out. I bit back a snort. Sebastian didn't bother, revealing his teeth in a wide grin.

"See? It's not just me!"

"Shut up," Calvin snapped. He lifted the point of the sword a little higher. The witch sucked in a sharp breath, then raised a crooked finger towards Calvin, the digit trembling, though I could not tell if it was in rage or with old age.

"You stole my heart and put it on your sword?" she asked, her voice quiet. "Like some trophy you won?"

"I did win, if you'll recall," Calvin said. "And I didn't even have to fight you to do it."

"This time you'll have to do more than smile," the witch hissed through her teeth. Then, she flew at Calvin.

Magic isn't really my thing, seeing as I'm pretty much human. Minus the Reaper part of me, that is, which isn't really magic as wizards and witches and sorcerers use it. So when I tell you that the witch struck at Calvin with both physical force and magic, assume that I am inadequately describing the sheer power of what she threw at my soul. There were sparks floating through the air like furious fireflies, surrounding currents of air that made the hair on the back of my neck stand up. The pieces I could see flared and waned like stars, a scythe of starstuff cutting through the Hut with ease.

Calvin, though, held his ground. He raised the sword and simply cut through the magic aiming for him. It splintered into thousands of shards of glass and fell to the ground. Then, it was his turn to attack, and he did so without hesitation. The sword moved through the air with speed and precision, cutting towards the witch's neck, her arms, her middle. She threw up magical defences to counter the attack, but Calvin was strong and furious.

And she hadn't counted on Sebastian. The magical debris that floated through the air was swiftly absorbed by the shadows that swarmed the air around him. His form became the darkest point in the shadows, an emptiness through which inevitability had to pass.

Except, that is, for his yellow eyes, which shone with a dark malice. Sebastian walked forwards with infinite calm while Calvin attacked with his magical sword, shadows eating the magic in the air, which left her open and defenceless.

The witch backed up a step. Two. Her eyes widened with fear and she raised an arm above her head to protect from attack. Her magic was not strong enough, though, to stop the point of the sword from digging into her skin. She began to bleed, a blue line of liquid trickling down her chest.

"See, Baba?" Calvin said with a smile. "I have learned since you saw me last, and even then I beat you. Now, you stand no chance at all. Your time is gone, witch. Time for you to give up on your cruelties and leave this world behind."

The sheer triumph in his voice hit me like a mallet. I sucked in a sharp breath and my thoughts began to swirl, like I'd taken some hallucinogen by accident. I saw myself, Calvin that is, in this same Hut, though the decor was rustic and homey rather than commercial and the windows hadn't been papered over. He was sitting at a table with this witch and a girl in folk garb, her golden hair bound in a scarf of the same colour as the witch. The three of them were sharing a meal.

My head started splitting. I ground my teeth and focused.

The meal turned to a game, possibly cards, though I saw a checkers set at one point. There were taunts exchanged. The girl quickly bowed out, some sort of light in her pocket whispering to her. Calvin continued. The taunting grew more intense, the emotion in the room thick enough to crackle like lightning.

Then, a deal was struck. One heart or the other, based on who would win the next hand. The girl tried to warn Calvin, the voice in her pocket telling him to leave, to walk away. Calvin remained.

And he won.

It was impossible, I knew it. I was exceptionally bad at card games—and board games for that matter—and had never really got the knack for them, either before Calvin and I split, or after. My soul would not have been any better than I was. He'd proven that by being on the losing end of the games for most of the night. But something happened, some sleight of hand, some trick, some bit of borrowed magic purchased in the Market, that let him win.

In essence, he cheated.

I cheated.

I'd done it before, sure. I was not above pulling a trick when it meant things were going to turn out for the best. But I had very particular rules about what constituted "the best" and cheating at a hand of cards for the sake of stealing a heart was not it.

A *thud* sounded through the fabric in my hands. My mind snapped back to the present and I realised that Death's heart was growing louder again. As it grew louder, so did my rage at my wayward soul. He'd called *me* the villain for my deeds. What about his?

This entire situation felt more than a little unfair on various sides. I was done with it, and the lies perpetrated by my soul. We were going to have a very firm talk about manners, and we were going to do it now.

I stood up from behind the table and stalked to the middle of the room.

"Cal, no!" Sebastian hissed.

The witch's eyes fixed on me, or more importantly, the bag in my hand. "What do you have there?" She licked her lips, even through the terror etched on her features.

"Stay back, witch, or I'll cut your head from your shoulders," Calvin warned. He stepped closer to her, the sword point aiming directly for the witch's heart. She smiled, revealing all of those pointed iron teeth.

"If you had the power to stop me, you would have done so already, *dushenka*. But you just stand there and wave that sword about. One measly cut? I will heal in minutes. So keep waving that sword, The sword protected with my heart, that you stole, see how futile your fight is. "

"I did not steal it," Calvin said. "I won it, and the protection it offered."

Why in the world would he need a witch's heart to protect him? It didn't matter.

"You did not win it," I interrupted. "You cheated."

The air in the room fell still as everyone processed my words. I felt the shadows that lived in Sebastian come alert, ready to explode outwards at a moment's notice. The witch stared at me with the preternatural stillness of those with magic running through their veins. Calvin turned to look at me over his shoulder, eyes wide with disbelief, as though I'd done something truly terrible by betraying his secret.

"Liar," he breathed, but the word lacked conviction.

"You called me the villain," I said. "You think that I am a terrible person for doing what I did to the dreaming giants and the exousia, for forcing Eddie to make his choice. You think that my coldness and my distance leave little room for doing the good thing, only facilitating the right thing. Well, perhaps you're right. But at least I am not a liar and a thief, like *you.*"

With a shout of fury, Calvin spun on his heel and lunged towards me. He was a better fighter with that sword than I expected. There was no hesitation as the blade met my chest. It was sharp, too, splitting the skin with no resistance. There was some as it hit bone, but whatever enchantment the witch's petrified heart granted the blade must have strengthened it, because my bone soon split as well.

My hands flexed reflexively and the bag dropped to the ground. I sucked in a breath. The jar shattered. I fell to my knees.

My movement wrenched the blade from Calvin's hands. Either that, or he was so shocked at what he'd done that he let go. Whichever it was, I now knelt on the ground, a sword in my chest, Death's heart beating fiercely on the ground, a bleeding and desperate witch before me, my traitorous soul staggering backwards in horror. Sebastian alone remained still, his dark eyes flicking between me and Calvin, as though he wasn't sure who to go to, who to believe.

I sucked in another breath.

I wouldn't regenerate until I pulled the sword from my chest, but I couldn't quite get my hands to move properly. They were twitching, not responding to my thoughts. That was probably due to the pain that was coursing through me, numbing me to everything but that fire.

"That heart," the witch breathed, shuffling a step forwards. "It cannot be."

"Cal," Sebastian said, voice pained. "Calvin."

The witch moved faster than I could imagine, lunging for me and the heart with her hands outstretched. As she moved, the Hut shifted also, tilting the floor towards her so that the heart would roll to her greedy fingers.

A hand slammed over the heart, stopping its movement. I realised a moment later that the hand was mine. Then, all coherent thought evaporated as I touched the vast well of power that lay in that artefact.

It was like the high I felt when gathering souls and lifeforce from the dead. It was a moment of feeling, true, unencumbered feeling, so pure and deep that it took my breath away. Before my eyes, the endless stars stretched out, their lights bright and blinding. In between the stars, I could feel the pulse of every living thing, the urge to be with them so intense that I was sure I would die from longing. Only, I could not die.

I would never die again.

I lifted the heart, that piece of the beautiful void, towards me with one hand. With the other, I pulled out the sword that pierced my chest. And, just as my vision began to flare white with my impending death and rejuvenation, I did the only thing that made perfect sense, and no sense at all. I put Death's heart into my own chest.

My wounds healed with my death, sealing the heart in. It would remain there until someone cut it out of me, if they could even fathom the sort of power it would take to subdue me and take that which was now mine.

The witch screamed, sliding backwards. Calvin and Sebastian ran towards me as if they were trying to stop me, though it was already too late. I felt the infinite void pulsing within me and I embraced it.

I held the sword in my hand, and I smiled.

"You are the witch known as Baba Yaga," I said, pointing the blade at the witch, who now looked like a frail old woman, her form speckled with silver life. "You are Elderkin, are you not?"

She quavered before me.

"Answer me!" I snapped, the sound filling the room.

"Yes," she said, lowering her gaze. "I am Elderkin."

"Good," I said. I walked towards her, wondering vaguely why she trembled as I approached. I held up the sword, the point facing the floor. "My soul stole this heart from you, and now I hold it in my hands. I could crush it like glass."

"I beg you, please, do not!" she yelped, instinctively reaching for the ruby. I held the sword away from her.

"What will you give to get it back? This is the Goblin Market, is it not?" I leaned in so that our faces were nearly touching and we could see the measure of the other in our eyes. "Let us make a bargain."

Baba Yaga, the witch, the Elderkin, swallowed, her throat bobbing, and nodded. "Yes," she breathed. "We bargain."

"Do you know where the resting place of the doomed is?"

She nodded.

"Cal, don't do this," Calvin said from over my shoulder. I ignored him, a cold fire flaring in my chest as I thought of his actions. It was not rage, but its counterpart in death, whatever it was. Emptiness and fire, mixing together in my blood as the heart beat steadily onwards beside my own.

"Shut up, Calvin," Sebastian growled. "He's got the right idea."

"Can you take us there?" I continued, ignoring both of my counterparts.

"Without detours or distractions, yes," the witch said, her voice breathless. She licked her lips, her eyes staring at the heart, pupils wide.

"Then, in exchange for you heart, do so."

I extended my hand to shake. She took it without hesitation. I felt the magic of a contract snap to life between us. Then, I handed over the heart and sword.

Calvin cried out a word in protest, but it was too late. The witch had already taken the stone from the hilt and shoved it in her mouth. She swallowed it, and a moment later magic flared up and filled the room. For an instant, her form flickered to that of a young woman like I'd seen in my soul's memories, then again to a pregnant woman hunched over her belly, then to the crone she showed herself to be. Only this time, the silver specks I saw in her became threads, twining together and strong. She tossed her head back and cackled.

With a sweep of her hand, the overturned furniture in the Hut righted itself. A stone mortar flew to her hand and she tossed it out the window, following a moment later. From outside, I heard her cry, "Come, now, Reaper! We fly!"

I looked out the window and found the witch in the mortar, now large and floating. She held out her hand, sparkling with magic, and I took it. Sebastian and Calvin shouted in protest. I turned back to look at them, and they both stiffened, then bowed their heads.

The witch and my three selves were flying over the lights and magic of the Goblin Market seconds later. I didn't care what my soul thought, or what Sebastian feared. I was going to get Neja and Agravane back, no matter what deals had to be struck.

If that truly did make me the villain, then so be it.

CHAPTER 12

Whether it was through the witch's magic, or her status as Elderkin, the journey over the Goblin Market lasted only a few minutes. The mortar landed in the midst of the graveyard, crunching dead plants beneath its weight. Sebastian leaped out, Calvin scrabbling close behind. I turned to Baba Yaga and inclined my head.

"This concludes our business, Reaper?" she asked, gnashing her iron teeth.

"It does." I stepped from the mortar onto the grass. The witch waved her hand and the mortar rose into the air. I could have sworn that I saw the ghost of that girl once again, so close to the witch that they could have been the same person. Instinctively, I knew they were not.

"If I ever see you or your soul again—" she started. I raised a hand, willing her to silence. Whatever power the heart granted me did just that, be it actual magic or the respect of those who favoured power above all else.

"You may try, if you feel so inclined," I said. "But it will not end any differently. It would be better if we just went out separate ways."

The witch wrinkled her nose, her teeth gleaming. Then, she nodded, dropping her gaze to the ground. I lowered my hand, letting the silence fall with it. The witch looked like she was going to speed off, the ghost in her wake.

"Do you know you're being haunted?" I asked, the words escaping before I could stop them. Baba Yaga's eyes flashed, those threads of silver power that ran through her flaring in alarm. The ghostly figure beside her flinched, eyes widening. She stared right at me. I stared back.

"After all this time..." the witch muttered. Then, turning a bright scarlet, she let out a hiss and steered her stone vessel into the air. "It is none of your concern, Reaper!"

"Very well," I said, inclining my head again. "Then our business is concluded."

She flew away from the graveyard without a backwards glance, her ghost going with her. A moment later I was tackled to the ground, and not by my own friendly griffin ghost, narrowly missing striking my head on a gravestone. No, this was Calvin's doing, and he was practically vibrating with anger.

My soul was a far better fighter than I was, but he was also emotional. Really, really emotional. Instead of subduing me as quickly as possible, he flailed with barely controlled violence. "You had no *right*!" he screamed, voice filling the empty graveyard. "You stole it! It was mine!"

His fist ploughed into my jaw and I nearly bit my tongue. My glasses went flying. I reared my head back and slammed my forehead into his nose. It gave a satisfying crack and Calvin cursed before going at me with fists flying, hitting every available surface.

I, as I have previously explained, am a terrible fighter. Oh, I got a few good hits in, sure; it was hard not to with him literally right on top of me. But he had far more passion than I did and the benefit of literal centuries of experience. If his fighting with the sword hadn't convinced me, this did. Calvin and I, we were most definitely not the same. We hadn't been for a very, very long time.

A shadow ripped the two of us apart, claws digging into flesh without consideration or mercy. It threw us apart and then stood between us while we dripped blood onto the ground. I recognised the manifestation of my Reaper abilities, all coils and teeth and claws. It was similar to a dragon, but so unlike it that the two would never be compared. Dragons were elegant, powerful creatures. This was a living nightmare of shadows and danger.

"Enough!" Sebastian's voice boomed across the yard. He lowered his head and snaked it between the two of us, fixing us with those enormous black eyes with yellow pupils. They slitted into pinpricks. "We are not here to act out your petty vendettas, little soul. Cal was in the right, giving the heart back to the witch. It got us here so we could rescue Agravane and Neja. Isn't that the most important thing?"

"You don't understand!" Calvin screamed. He paced in a tight circle, tearing at his hair. My soul-inflicted wounds were already beginning to heal, so I sat up, brushing dirt off. I reached and found my glasses. The left lens had cracked, but otherwise they were whole enough to see through. The desperation in my soul's expression came into focus.

"Then explain it," I growled.

Calvin rounded on me. "Have you *any* idea what it's like to wander the realms for centuries as nothing more than pure soul? How much energy I contain? How many people would be happy to devour me? That heart was my only protection. The only thing strong enough to keep me safe."

"You stole it. You cheated," I said. My veins flooded with that same empty rage as before, though less strongly. It was a disconcerting sensation, like having emotions again, but no emotion I'd ever felt. I could, however, feel the void full of stars pounding with each intake of breath. I could feel the infinite sparks of life that existed in that void, and I wished for each and every one.

"As if you wouldn't have done the same," Calvin spat. "You've cheated, too."

"To save the entire mortal realms!" I said, standing and brushing myself off. "Not for some simple self-serving gain."

"Self-serving?" My soul took an exaggerated step

backwards, his hand pressed to his chest in melodramatic hurt. "Protection is self-serving?"

"When you cannot die, yes," I said. Calvin stared at me like I'd suddenly grown two heads. He took another step backwards, this time not exaggerated.

"You…you actually believe that? Without even hearing my full story? Without knowing what it was that I went through?" he asked, voice quiet yet sharp enough to cut through the air.

"The memory I saw was one of a man proving that he had the ability to cheat and steal and deceive someone more powerful than he, not someone who was afraid." Indeed, the memory had been tainted with glee at his success, not worry about being devoured. He'd been confident enough to risk losing over and over and over again.

Calvin sucked in a breath. "The memory you saw?"

"Obviously, the connection goes both ways," Sebastian said. He pulled the shadowy coils together and stepped towards the both of us, back to his human form. He tugged at the sleeves of his shirt. "While this blame game has been extremely diverting, I think perhaps we should focus on trying to find our missing friends, wouldn't you agree?"

Calvin and I eyed each other. I wasn't sure what my soul would do when he was backed into a corner, and it was fairly clear he thought the same. A blue blur shattered our stare down, ghostly feathers flashing as Tempest appeared from wherever she'd been hiding all this time. She rubbed against Sebastian's legs like a cat, arching her back merrily. She flicked her tail at Calvin and launched herself into the air, winging around my head twice before landing on my shoulder. Then, she bit my ear.

I flinched. "Ow."

Tempest chattered at me, rubbing her head against my face. Calvin scoffed. "I don't know why you're so attached to the creature, anyways. What help is she?"

Tempest hissed at Calvin, then threw herself off my shoulder and started flying towards the wall surrounding the graveyard, diving in and out of the solid stone until I got the message. She wanted us to follow her. She was still on the scent trail of Agravane and Neja.

"She's the best tracker I know," I said. "And better company than some people." I followed after Tempest, not really caring whether Calvin and Sebastian were with me. I went through the door as I had before, entering into that strange, dark forest full of whispers. As soon as my feet touched the moss and clover ground cover, the whispers stopped.

Tempest let out a screech that echoed through the trees, a challenge to those wisps of the Elderkin. I was tempted to echo the sentiment, but managed to refrain. Barely. Sebastian stepped up to my side and a reluctant Calvin stood on his other side. Then, we started walking through the forest.

I wasn't terribly good with navigation, especially not in a dark forest with trees that looked almost exactly the same, but I could have sworn that we weren't going the same way as before. They'd moved my friends. Tempest was easily able to track them, which was very good. The thought of these beings harming Agravane and Neja, though, was enough to have me clenching my fists, the void inside of me flaring with energy. I began walking faster.

The three of me—of us? Talking in triplicate was proving difficult—didn't bother saying anything as we went. I could feel Sebastian's shadows moving about, wake and wary. Calvin's anger was practically pulsing off of him in waves. Good. We would need it.

The trees thinned out into a clearing lit with tiny wisps of bobbing light. Will-o-wisps, if I wasn't mistaken, though they could have just been flames suspended in the tree tops. The ground was covered in soft clover and the occasional patch of ferns and nettles. The sky was almost completely black, enough so that I couldn't see the descending stones of the Market, if we were even still there.

Tempest flew straight into the clearing then back again, landing on my shoulder and kneading the fabric of my shirt with her claws. She purred.

"Well done," I said, scratching her behind the ear. It was so like touching real feathers and fur that I could almost pretend that she wasn't dead, that her last tracking mission hadn't ended badly for so many. I hesitated at the edge of the trees. How many more of my decisions would go badly? Perhaps I was wrong about Calvin, about our differences. He was my soul, after all. Shouldn't I give him the benefit of the doubt?

"It's a henge," Sebastian said, interrupting yet another of my internal rabbit hole monologues. I blinked, my thoughts returning to the present, and the fact that I had to rescue Agravane and Neja as quickly as possible. My Reaper abilities were correct. Before us was a henge, a bank surrounding a slight depression in the ground rising up to a flat top encircled with standing stones. Stones that looked to be made of diamond.

"This place is dangerous," Calvin murmured. He reached a hand over the bank and ditch, into the air of the henge, and shivered. "It's a trap. Meant for the magical and those with enough power to defeat this place."

"Are you sure?" I asked. I was tempted to reach forward as well, but I doubted that doing so blindly, with Death's heart beating in my chest, would be a good idea.

Calvin shot me a dark look. "I'm sure. I've seen enough traps in my existence to recognise one."

"Tempest, are you certain that Neja and Agravane are there?" Sebastian asked, reaching out to scratch the griffin's ears. She chirped and ducked her head in an approximation of a nod. Yes, she was certain. My Reaper half and I exchanged a glance, his dark eyes more determined than worried.

"Very well, then," I said. "Let's go get ourselves caught, shall we?"

Then, I took a step into the clearing. Calvin lunged for me, wrapping his hands around my arm and pulling me backwards. "Are you *insane*?!"

"They are holding my friends," I snapped. "Our friends, unless you are truly so different that you can't acknowledge that much. These fools think that they've got us dead to rights. They want to catch us. Me. They want to catch me. And if that's the only way to get Agravane and Neja back, then I'll get caught."

"And if they drain your power? If they carve open that chest of yours and pull out your hearts?" Calvin was openly glaring, now, but I recognised the concern for what it was. The only question was whether it was concern for me, or concern for him.

"They're certainly welcome to try," I said. Sebastian chuckled.

"Come on, little soul, you know full well that any force that chooses to oppose us is foolish at best."

"Are you calling me foolish?" Calvin snapped. He adjusted his own glasses and stared down Sebastian.

The shadows beneath the Reaper's skin came to life, writhing about and dancing in the half-light of the wisps. He lunged forwards, faster than I could see, and grabbed Calvin's arm, his shadows attaching themselves to my soul. Then, he grabbed my arm, those shadows doing the same to me, though I got the impression it was a show for Calvin's benefit. With a forceful tug, I was pulled across the ditch and into the henge.

A fierce hum filled the air, like electric lights at a concert. The diamond stones flared to life, their energy pulsing a bright red. Sebastian let Calvin and I go, raising his hands in surrender.

"Oh, dear. We've been caught. Whatever will we do?" he deadpanned.

Calvin raised his hands as well. "This had better work," he muttered under his breath. "If it doesn't, I'm blaming you."

"Yes, yes, it's always my fault," I grumbled in return, lifting my hands into the air.

At our surrender, the henge stones flashed orange, bright enough to blind. I blinked rapidly to clear my vision of spots. We'd been transported. Wherever this was, it was certainly not a henge. It looked more like a dungeon or a cave, with enormous stone blocks covered in lichens and moss making up the walls, the only light coming from a fiercely glowing box on a pedestal and Tempest still on my shoulder. Chains rattled off to my left and I whirled, the light barely bright enough to show me Agravane chained to a wall, his arms outstretched just above head height.

"Cal," he wheezed, grinning at me. "What a coincidence, seeing you here."

"You look like crap," I said. And he did, his skin sallow and bruised, his hair wet and matted. It had only been a couple of days by my calendar, but I had travelled between realms and through the Market more than a few times. I had no idea how long he'd actually been down here, chained. Possibly tortured.

"Yes, well, they're out of hot water and you know how much I hate cold showers. And..." He closed one eye, then the other, before blinking a few times. "And there are three of you?"

"Indeed," Calvin drawled, his displeasure apparent. "I told you so!"

"Cal?" Agravane asked. "Why are you talking in an American accent?"

"Do you know, I wondered the same thing. Now let's see about getting you down from there."

CHAPTER 13

I gave Agravane a very, very truncated version of what had happened over the last couple of hours or days or however long it had actually been. Sebastian chimed in on occasion, adding an important detail or clarifying something. Calvin remained silent, leaning against a wall in the corner, sulking.

"These chains are really stuck," I said, doing my best to pull them from the wall. I'd tried bashing them open with a rock, prying them apart, and was now trying to wiggle them free from the stone itself.

"Too bad we don't have a sword," Calvin muttered. Sebastian pointed at him.

"Shut up unless you feel like being helpful."

Agravane's mouth twitched in what I really hoped was amusement. "This is bizarre. It's like every aspect of your personality mirrored and multiplied. I can't wait to tell Yolanda about this."

"Well, you'll have to wait until we can figure out

how to get you out of here," I grumbled. My rock troll assistant would have an absolute field day with this. "By the way, where's Neja?"

Agravane nodded his head towards the glowing box on the plinth in the middle of the room. "They bound her to the box, took away her corporeal form. Like the legends of old, the djinns trapped in lamps."

I whirled to face the glowing box. It pulsated with an orangey energy that was almost like fire. As I focused on it, I could have sworn that the colour darkened and the energy seemed to intensify. She was pissed. "Oh, crap," I said. "How do I get her out?"

Agravane waggled his fingers. "Like the legends of old, Cal. Duh."

I looked at Sebastian for clarification. He just shrugged. Calvin pushed himself away from the wall and stalked towards the box. Then, with a flourish that was more melodramatic than dramatic, he rubbed his hand over the side of the box as if cleaning it.

Immediately, the box burst apart, shards of glass flying through the room. I ducked and yelped. Sebastian just stepped aside as a piece flew towards his face. Calvin got a couple of cuts, but nothing major. In the place of the box, though, was a figure. It was humanoid, but made of smoke and embers, with eyes like live coals. Still, it was definitely Neja; the scowl she wore was signature.

"You're okay!" I said, rushing forwards and wrapping my arms around her. Somehow, she was solid enough to touch, but the tighter I hugged, the more ephemeral she felt. Eventually I pulled back. "Why aren't you…?"

"Solid?" Neja spat. "It's a side effect of being bound like that. I can appear human, but only with the permission of the one who freed me. Oh, by the way—" She spun to face Calvin and gave an exaggerated bow. "Thank you, great sir, for freeing me from the, ah, box. You have been granted three wishes, so that I may repay your kindness."

"What?" Calvin asked.

"What?!" I screeched.

"Is that three wishes to Calvin, or one to each of us, since we are all Cal?" Sebastian asked, crossing his arms and lifting his chin. Trust him to get to the nuance of a situation moments after it happened. Sheesh. Neja blinked, her eyes sparking. She looked between the three of me. Her mouth worked and the embers floating through her form glowed brightly.

"Don't ruin this for me, Reaper," Calvin snarled. "I've been apart from Cal for centuries. That means we're separate people."

"Actually, I'm not sure," Neja admitted, which was a first for her. She wavered, her form fluctuating as she thought. "I've never encountered a single being split apart like this, and as far as I know none of my kindred have either, or there would be something in my magic telling me how to proceed."

"I'm the one who freed you, I should get the wishes," Calvin said. He was looking a little desperate, his fingers twitching. I had no idea what he would wish for if he could, but I doubted it would be good. At least, not for me.

"Neja," I said, holding my hand out to her. Surprisingly, she took it, though we couldn't do more than imitate holding hands, what with her being incorporeal. "Are you okay?"

"I've been bound, Cal, what do you think?" she asked, but there was a slight smile in her smokey mouth. Calvin reached for her.

"My wishes!" he demanded. "You have to grant me my wishes!"

Neja recoiled. "This is your soul?" she hissed.

"Yeah. He's got a bit to learn about manners."

As soon as I said that, though, Calvin lunged, reaching for Neja like she was a lifeline in a storm. Neja pulled back, but I knew a little about djinn magic from when we'd first met in Chicago. She had to obey her master for as long as she was subjugated—that is until the wishes were fulfilled—and she couldn't really flee. So Calvin grabbed her smokey wrist and pulled, and even incorporeal, Neja had to comply.

I felt what little control I had slipping, and then I was leaping for my soul. This time, though, I was doing so with the power of the void at my disposal, with the death of stars at my fingertips. We really needed to stop fighting, but I couldn't seem to bring myself to pull back. I grabbed Calvin's face and where my fingers touched his flesh, dark lines appeared. They stretched outwards, curling and spreading along his skin towards his eyes, his neck. He screamed.

Then, I felt a shattering pain in my own face. I retreated, scrabbling at the skin there and feeling lines along my cheek, my jaw. I couldn't hurt Calvin, even now. He was my soul, and what damage I had tried to do to him was simply reflected back on myself. Death's heart granted me severe power, but I couldn't use it on Calvin.

And he still held Neja.

"Cal," she breathed, staring at me with wide, ember-filled eyes. "What did you do?"

I rubbed my chest where I could feel Death's heart beating and grimaced. "Another time."

"Perhaps we can discuss the situation like adults," Sebastian suggested, voice ripe with anger. "We need to free Agravane and figure out how to get out of here. After all, someone trapped us here intentionally, and I doubt they are going to leave us alone for long."

Calvin's eyes sparked with fear and he shifted his weight. His hand tightened on Neja's wrist, nearly slipping through her smoke. "I could wish us free," he said in a low voice. There was something desperate in the way he said that. "Ask me to wish us free."

"No," I said.

"Calvin, this is really not the time to work out your grudge towards Cal," Sebastian snapped. "Like it or not, we are all the same person, even if only a piece of him. We need to cooperate!"

"He stole my protection, ruined my life at the tea shop, has driven me insane with those *dreams*—"

"What you dream is not my fault," I said.

"Shut up!" Calvin screamed.

"Uh, Cal," Agravane whispered from behind me. "This may not be the best time—"

"It's really not," I agreed, ignoring him. "Calvin, look. Giving Baba Yaga back her heart was the best way to get us here. You agreed that we needed to rescue Agravane and Neja. What would you have us do, take several days or even weeks to get back here? What state would they be in then?"

Calvin hesitated. Just a touch, but I could tell he was hesitating.

"You have no idea what I've been through," he muttered. His fingers loosened enough that Neja was able to slip free. She flitted across the room to stand by Agravane, for what little protection that offered.

"I don't," I answered. "I really don't. But you can tell me about it, and maybe I'll get another of those memory-vision things. It'll be like all the dreams you've had. Right?"

Calvin eyed me, cradling his hands against his body. He looked around the room, looking a fraction longer at Neja than at anyone else. Then, he looked at me. And, in perhaps the greatest mistake I've made in a while, I looked back. Our gazes locked. Even with all the power thrumming through my veins, I could not break away from the look that Calvin gave me, and I had a feeling he could not look away either.

The world around me vanished, leaving me in that same white plane I visited when I died. Calvin stood across from me. He opened his mouth to speak. Before he could, the white plane shifted. I screamed, unable to stop myself as my mind was overrun with a thousand images and a tidal wave of emotion like I hadn't felt since my soul was cleaved from my body. I saw people live, and die as Calvin—as I—neither aged nor changed. I saw relationships form and then crumble when I had to steal away in the middle of the night. I saw the naked lust that lived in the eyes of those magical beings who knew what I was, what power I held in my form. I felt claws tearing me to shreds over and over again as I died and returned. I saw civilisations fall and empires rise. I saw wars stretching endlessly across the horizon. All through this, I felt every ounce of emotion a person could feel, unable to regulate it at all. Unable to push past it and think rationally. I was driven wholly by the unfettered *feeling* that consumed me until I was so exhausted I could do nothing but collapse.

I saw it all. I felt it all. And I screamed.

In the time that I'd been without a soul, I'd become hyperrational, even cold, indifferent about so many things in life because I could not bind them with emotion. In the much longer time that Calvin had been separate from me, he had the opposite problem. He was a live wire, pure and raw emotion without anything else. And he'd gone insane from the horror of feeling the world fully.

Finally, the vision ran out, or I managed to close my eyes or something. I fell to my knees, my fingers clawing at my hair. I squeezed my eyes shut and took several deep breaths. Already, the overwhelming flood of emotion was fading, leaving me with a sense of disquiet and the knowledge that my soul was well and truly insane. He hadn't wanted protection because he could be hurt; he'd wanted protection so the world would leave him alone.

Vaguely I realised that people were shouting my name. I took another deep breath and opened my eyes. Agravane was straining against the chains, looking like he was trying to reach me by any means necessary. Neja was holding him back, streaks of fire on her smokey cheeks: her tears in this form. Sebastian circled me, his dark eyes cunning and watchful. Calvin huddled in the corner, his knees brought up to his chin, rocking back and forth as he sobbed.

"Never again," he pleaded, looking at me through a film of snot and tears. "Never again."

"Never again," I promised him, though I wasn't sure how I could possibly fulfil that. I didn't even know how to get him or Sebastian back in my body. I couldn't even free us from this place. I managed to stand, barely, and leaned against one of the stone walls while my legs regained feeling.

"What was that?" Neja demanded. "What happened?"

"I…saw the memories of my soul," I said. My voice was hoarse, as if I'd been shouting for hours. I might have been, for all I knew. "He had centuries of memories, and I saw them all."

"Why were you screaming?" Agravane asked, relaxing his struggle against the chains. "Cal, you sounded like you were dying."

"I can't die," I said automatically, but I didn't necessarily disagree. Though, feeling the precise moment one loses their mind is nothing at all like dying. I would know. It's like shattering into a thousand pieces, each one aware of the other but unable to do anything coherent.

"Cal," Agravane said again. He licked his dry lips. His shoulders sagged and his breathing was heavy.

"He went insane," I said flatly. "While I was working for Death, doing jobs and running errands, my soul went insane."

Silence filled the air for a moment. Then, Sebastian clapped me on the shoulder. I turned to find him unable to meet my gaze, as if afraid he would see the same things I had seen if he looked too closely. "Let's test my theory about the wishes," he said, startling me.

Ah, yes, the three wishes. Hard to care about a thing like that in the face of the knowledge that your very core, the very thing that makes you, you, is broken, crazy.

"Neja," Sebastian said with a polite bow of his head. "If you please, I wish for Agravane to be freed from the chains which bind him to the wall."

A flash of light filled the air, like fire, and I heard the rattling of chains. When my vision cleared, Agravane was slumped on the floor, taking in great lungfuls of air. He rubbed the skin on his wrists where the chains had dug in. "Thank you," he rasped.

"You are welcome," Sebastian said. Then he turned to me. "It would appear that each of us does indeed have a wish."

"Then I wish we were out of this dungeon!" Calvin's voice cracked across the room and I winced. Before I could ask that he take it back, reword the wish to something more precise, something that couldn't be twisted by whatever dark requirements Neja's magic had, the room flared into fire again.

When the brightness cleared this time, the dungeon had fallen away. We were back at the henge, the crystal stones alight with power. It felt good to breathe in fresh air, even if for a moment. Before I could do more than think that thought, several figures appeared.

They were ghostly, not quite solid and yet not the shimmering blue of Tempest's feathers. No, these figures were wreathed in gold, their eyes brimming with it, their hair made of it. They wore garb of several different cultures and times. Some had the draped, diaphanous clothes of Rome or Greece, while others wore something more shaped, but with turbans and bare chests. Still others had wild eyes and beads twined into their thick locks of hair. I recognised none of them, but then why would I?

These were the Elderkin, after all. The former deities who wandered around, not quite able to die, but forgotten. Their power base was gone, except for this tiny proving ground in the corner of the Goblin Market. Here, where heroes presided and the rest perished, these gods still had power.

And most of it was directed straight at me.

CHAPTER 14

A woman wearing a long dress and a mantle of fur, her hair wild and riotous, took a tiny step forwards and lifted her chin. "We meet at last, hero who is not a hero."

We were going to be dramatic, then. "Yes. Hello. Nice to meet you. Now that the pleasantries are over, I'll be taking my friends and leaving, thanks."

The woman scoffed with a practised toss of her head. "Leaving? Oh, no, human, I don't think so. It's been centuries since we last had a hero wander through our test, and now we are met with you, who come through here twice in less than a week? Who are escorted the second time by Baba Yaga herself? You escaped our dungeon with ease, you tamed our leviathan, and killed our manticore. Yet you think you can just leave?"

I sighed. "Sebastian, would you care to deal with this?"

He chuckled. "No, I'm enjoying watching you."

Neither one of us asked Calvin, and he seemed content to cower behind Agravane and Neja, eyeing the Elderkin warily. So I brushed off some of the dirt from my now tattered clothes, gave Tempest a scratch under her chin, and straightened my glasses.

Then, because these people seemed to respond well to drama, I said in my coldest voice, "Do you honestly think that you can stop me?"

That set the Elderkin off. They started murmuring amongst themselves. Those that were armed drew their weapons and brandished them. A couple took threatening steps forwards. In another moment, they would start a brawl, just to see who could attack me first. These people had likely not seen any defiance in centuries, and here I was, full of snark and just prime for a thrashing. The leader raised her hand and the forgotten gods stilled.

"Do you know who I am?" she sneered at me. I shrugged irreverently. Nostrils flaring, she held her hands out and said in a firm declaration, "I am Katir, goddess of battles long lost and wars won before the realms were split apart. I have seen things you could not even imagine and fought in hopeless situations that would have you screaming in horror. I am a warrior of warriors and you cannot stand before me!"

I sighed, wishing I had a watch to check, just to show my indifference. "Honestly, lady, you're not even the scariest thing I've seen all day."

No, that would have been the thoughts swirling

through my soul's mind. But she didn't need to know that.

Katir staggered backwards. She clenched her jaw and glared, and had she been at her full power, at the height of her reign and followed by her acolytes, then maybe I would have quaked. As it was, despite my show of indifference, I felt a bit badly for her. For all of them. They were so desperately clinging to glory that had abandoned them long ago. They were shadows—literally—of their former selves. They glowed gold, sure, but if I were to look at them with my Reaper sense, I had no doubt that their lifeforces would be mostly all-too-mortal yellow.

They were dying.

And I was likely going to be the one to kill them.

Any defiance at this point would be enough to do them in, to send their spirits scattering to the winds. I could probably pluck their lifeforces from their bodies with a single touch, should I have my Reaper abilities activated. Sebastian, though, was refraining from getting involved, and for good reason. It was sad. They didn't deserve to be ended in such a pathetic display.

One of the Elderkin garbed in long robes with intricate embroidery leaped for me, his glowing sword heading straight for my neck. I made no move to stop him, even knowing how much pain it would cause to be decapitated. His sword cut through the air like water, then came for me. The flare of agony burned. I could feel my skin and bone splitting, then I felt nothing. The familiar burst of white came as I died and rejuvenated, and I took a moment to catch my breath. The empty plane was normally quiet and peaceful, a place of stillness before I returned to the world and the reality of my deathless self, but this time there was no peace to be found. I saw specks of black filling the white plane. It was like looking at the night sky in reverse, with black stars and white sky, and I had a feeling it did note bode well for me. I felt that desperate longing I associated with Death's heart; it pounded through my veins and my head, irresistible, overwhelming.

Then, the moment was gone. I was pulled back to the henge, alive and whole, if disconcerted by the scene I'd just witnessed. I pulled off my glasses and cleaned the blood from them, shoved the confusion over my experience in the empty plane away, then looked at the Elderkin. They were staring at me with open-mouthed horror.

"Anyone else care to try?" I asked, doing my best to be gentle.

"What *are* you?" Katir asked.

"My name is Cal Thorpe, and I am a marketing agent," I said. The Elderkin looked confused, some more horrified, as if the words I spoke were the equivalent of some ancient terror that they'd never faced before and had hoped never to meet in open battle. "I promote people's images, make you well known on all the social media platforms, in conversation, in life. I sell people, products, ideas, so that others will want to participate and learn and be involved, if only through observation. I can make your names known again throughout the realms. You would no longer be forgotten gods. You would be remembered, known, seen, heard. If you let me help you."

"Cal, what are you doing?" Calvin asked. He was still cowering behind Agravane and Neja, both of whom were staying wisely quiet and out of the fight. The aurai likely because he knew what I could do as a marketing agent and the djinn likely because she knew what I could do if the Elderkin refused my offer.

My soul, on the other hand, had no such restraint. "They tried to kill us, and you're offering to market for them? They kidnapped Agravane and Neja! They want to destroy us!"

"Shut up, Calvin," Sebastian snarled. "Or I will muzzle you."

"They're a threat!" Calvin insisted. "They've already hurt Agravane and—"

"Enough," I murmured. Immediately, both Calvin and Sebastian backed down, though I could feel the tension in the air. I looked at Katir and the others surrounding her, whose gazes were beginning to show fear more than horror. I wasn't sure which was worse.

"Well?" I looked at each of them. "Do you accept my offer?"

"Why would you do this for us?" Katir asked, a desperate sneer painting her lips. "Do you think we are fools to fall at your feet for a dream that we've long since abandoned? The world left us behind long ago. No one can do what you say, not for us!"

I shook my head. "I can, and I would. I market for Death. I sell the best coffee in Elsewhere. I have

Dwarven empires on my client list. I do all this, and more. And I would offer it to you."

Katir narrowed her eyes. She crossed her arms, hugging her waist tightly. "Why? Why would you offer such a thing?"

"Because, if you do not let me and my friends leave without incident, I will be forced to fight you, and you will lose. Your existence will end, and it will be my doing." I offered my hands in supplication. "I do not wish to do this, but I will. And I will not feel regret, or guilt, or sorrow, or horror, or anything at all. You will be dead, more than forgotten, and your killer won't even feel for you."

"You could not do such a thing." The Elderkin who had attacked me scoffed, though his grip on his sword was white-knuckled and his eyes were panicked.

"I could," I said. "I am a Reaper. I am the giver of choices. I am the one in between Life and Death, between yes and no, between the todays and tomorrows. And the choice I give you is this: release me and my friends, and I will market for you so that people remember your names, so that your power might return in some small measure; or do not, and I will fight you."

Katir hesitated. She looked at the Elderkin on either side of her. Some were nodding, others shaking their heads, still others perfectly still. Then, in a very calculated move, she straightened her shoulders, lifted her chin and looked down at me with all the self-assuredness of a god, forgotten or otherwise.

"I must say, Cal Thorpe, I *am* impressed," she

purred. "You have caused more dissent than most heroes who make it this far. Instead of bending the knee, you choose to sow discord amongst us."

I sighed. It was going to be like that, then. A pity.

In a blur of motion, she leaped for me, putting her hands around my throat. Though every instinct I had was telling me to flail madly at her and then run away —something I was quite good at, thank you—I remained still, my muscles relaxed. Katir inhaled, taking in my scent, then leaned in so her mouth was at my ear.

"Your sheer arrogance is astounding," she breathed. My heart sank. Death's heart began to beat faster, as if it knew what was coming next. "To threaten a *god*."

"It was not a threat," I said on a rasp, her fingers a little tight for comfortable speech. "It was fact."

"I'm amazed at how deluded you are. Then, you've had so many successes in our little maze. It's no wonder you feel so strong, so capable. Now tell me, human or marketing agent or Reaper or whatever you really are, how does it feel to be so powerless? To have my hands at your throat?"

"Your friend took my head, and here I stand."

Katir tightened her grip. I could feel my airways close and saw spots behind my eyes. It was getting harder not to struggle, but it wouldn't do any good. I was a terrible fighter and this was some ancient goddess of war. She would kill me, as surely as her friend had. It wouldn't matter.

"Don't hurt him!" Calvin screamed, his voice a half-sob.

"Calvin, relax," Sebastian growled. "He will be fine!"

Calvin was incoherent, shouting and demanding Katir stop, crying like a toddler. I knew, now, that he'd experienced so much pain, so many deaths, that the thought of any more was appalling to him, enough to set off a violent panic attack. Something fundamental in him had cracked, and now he was watching me—watching *himself*—suffer.

I couldn't do that to my own soul, no matter how much I disliked or didn't understand him.

I brought my hand up to Katir's chest, where her neck and torso met. She tightened her grip further and the spots became more intense. I knew I was going to pass out at any moment. I closed my eyes, let my body relax, and delved into the beating heart that I bore which was not my own.

Death's heart responded eagerly.

I had felt that impossible longing since taking the heart into my chest, but now I gave in. The desire for the light surrounding those multitudes of stars in the void roared to life. It consumed me, spreading shadows and emptiness through every vein, every vessel in my body. I felt it surge up and leech through my skin, pouring out of me in hungry waves. It touched the first living thing around me and began to devour in exquisite joy.

The power Katir had left in her lifeforce was negligible compared to some of the beings I'd met, but she was still Elderkin. Her might may have diminished over the millennia, but it was still enough to send shocks of energy, euphoria, through me. It filled every empty hole in me that I hadn't even known existed, and for the first time in...*ever*, I felt whole. I was incandescent.

Katir, on the other hand, was devoured. Her hands, where they wrapped around my throat, became spider-webbed with shadow. The devouring parasite spread, twisting and twining its way up her body then spreading until it covered her entirely. Her form pulsated once. She screamed. Then, she just vanished into dust.

I pulled back from that insatiable desire as the high of taking Katir's lifeforce faded. It was like waking up after a perfect nap, where I was unable to face reality and yet determined to do so. My hand fell, dust sliding off my skin.

Dimly, I became aware that Calvin was still sobbing in the background, though the noise was more frightened than it was panicked and inconsolable. I didn't turn to see the looks on the faces of my two counterparts and my two friends. Instead, I looked at the remaining Elderkin. They were huddled together, what weapons they had pointed at me as if that would do anything to stop me, should I choose to attack.

"You killed her," the robed man with the sword said, his golden light flickering with fear. "You *killed* an Elderkin!"

"I gave her a choice." I brushed some more dust off my skin. "She chose her fate."

"You were lying! A trick by a hero to try and outsmart the gods!" This was from a short woman with a hunched back and only one eye. She leaned on a staff twice her height, legs trembling.

"I am sorry if that is what you believe, but I was not lying. I have just proven to you that I wasn't lying."

"He tamed your leviathan, navigated your maze, killed your manticore, and escaped your dungeon." I was surprised to hear Sebastian's voice at my shoulder. But the Reaper part of me stood at my right. And, even more shockingly, Calvin stood at my left, his arms wrapped around his middle, righteous anger burning in his eyes. "He did all these things, came back from the dead, and yet you still thought he was lying? It would appear that you were all forgotten for the simple reason that you are fools."

The Elderkin clustered tighter together, and for the first time since coming to this henge, I could sense their absolute desperation. It was reaching a boiling point, and the next few moments could decide their entire future. Or their end.

"I offer you the choice again," I said, keeping my posture relaxed even as I prepared to delve into that terrible power once more. "Let me and mine go, and I will do my best to return your names to the world. Or fight, and die."

They watched me, silent. I watched them, waiting.

Finally, expression set in a line of determination, the robed man raised his sword.

I closed my eyes. "I see."

"Cal," Sebastian murmured, putting his hand on my arm. I shrugged it off.

"Neja, I know my wish."

"Okay, Cal," she said, and her voice was steady in a way that mine was not.

"I wish to give these Elderkin a peaceful end. As much as can be done, that is."

"Okay, Cal," Neja said again. I felt her wish magic flare. I delved into that void once more. And the world turned to shadow.

CHAPTER 15

My left hand had gone completely numb. I noticed it as soon as we left the crystal henge. Tempest flew around my head, winging close, but not quite landing on my shoulder. Her eyes were wide and her stump of a tail was fluffed out. I can't imagine that my display of power was pleasant for her.

"It's alright, Tempest," I said as she flew closer. I tried to lift my left arm and managed it, but my hand was limp and my forearm was tingling. I stared at the limb and tried to move it again, flexing my fingers. I couldn't. I looked at the others.

Neja, now in her humanoid form after completing the three wishes, still looking a bit worse for wear, approached with a frown. She took my hand and inspected it. I couldn't feel a thing. "Cal?" she asked, running her bluish-grey fingers over my palm. "Anything?"

I shook my head.

"This is bad," Sebastian said, suddenly standing at my right shoulder. I yelped and pulled away, only to run into Calvin, who was staring at my hand with a frightening intensity.

"It's getting worse," Calvin said, his earlier instability now replaced with a flat, solemn, even dangerous affect. "The separation between us. The fading."

"The fact that we're literally standing right next to each other isn't helping?" I was severely annoyed by this. It seemed like something Fate should have mentioned when she was reuniting us. Not that Death's mother had been at all helpful in any way, shape, or form.

"Your use of Death's heart likely didn't help matters," Agravane said. He, too, picked up my hand. Instead of looking it over, he just dropped it; my reflexes and muscles were too slow to catch it and it flopped at my side. "The fading is getting worse. You've overextended yourself and having you in three separate pieces means you can't bounce back like you would otherwise. I've seen this sort of thing when magic users burn themselves out. It never ends well."

"We have to find Fate, get her to put us back together." As one, we all turned to stare at Calvin. He flinched, hunching his shoulders and glaring at us. "What? It's true."

"It is," I agreed.

"We just never thought you would be the one to suggest it," Sebastian said.

Calvin's scowl deepened. He folded his arms and

slouched like a petulant teenager. "Do you know what it's like being me? I thought I was normal, coping with everything for so long. Then you lot show up and… and…and it's like looking in the mirror of what I could have been and realising that I'm not normal! I'm crazy. I get it. I've lost my mind and there's nothing I can do about it. Except get put back together with you."

Sebastian took a deep breath. He nodded. "I agree. While I am not, ah, in mental distress due to the separation, I know my capacity as a Reaper has been diminished. That, and I would very much like not to die."

"Me, too," I said. "I also don't want to die."

"So it's decided," Neja said. "We go find Fate, like we were meant to do on this ridiculous quest to begin with."

"Yes, I do apologise for the detour," I said. "You weren't meant to get kidnapped and, er, dematerialised."

Neja stiffened for a moment, then sighed. "You contracted for my services. That means I face the consequences. Though my hazard pay clause kicked in, so expect a hefty compensation fee." Her banter, such as it was, felt flat.

No matter what Neja and I seemed to do, we never could catch a break. It was probably time for me to let her go her own way, to live her life without my interference. She would be better off. I schooled my features into my most professional expression and nodded.

"Of course. Send me your invoice when you return home, and I will be sure it's paid promptly." Even as I said the words, Neja frowned. Her frown turned into anger that caught her eyes on fire and made them blaze. She strode forwards, lifted her arm, and slapped me soundly across the face.

"What was that for?" Calvin demanded.

"Cal was being an idiot, obviously," Sebastian sighed. "Though I don't generally condone violence in such occasions, I will say that this was warranted."

"Don't condone violence?" Calvin parroted. "Since when?"

"Will you two shut up?" Agravane snapped. He pinched the bridge of his nose. "Dealing with one of you was bad enough. This is absurd. Next time, Yolanda gets to babysit you."

"You *are* being an idiot," Neja said, hands on hips and eyes fierce. "Do you honestly think that, after *everything* we've been through, I would be content with just going home and, what, sending you my bill?"

I scratched my jaw. "Honestly, yes. I assumed that things were—"

Neja threw her hands up. "Things are *always* crazy around you, Cal Thorpe! That's what makes you so infuriating. You're so…so…ugh."

"Oblivious," Agravane said. "That's the word you want."

Neja narrowed her eyes at him and he put his hands up, walking away. She turned back to me. "I got into this bounty hunter and mercenary business because it was fun in a world that basically sucks. But you, from the first time we met—"

"After you dropped a piano on me."

"Yes, Cal, after I dropped a piano on you." Neja rolled her eyes. "You have been a proverbial thorn in my side. Stupid, oblivious to the ways of the world, absolutely naïve when it comes to social interactions, and annoyingly capable. You're cunning in ways you shouldn't be. You don't do things normally, but you always get things done. And when you have enough power to tear the entire world to shreds, you wish to make the death of lost gods *peaceful.* Do you know how annoying that is?!"

I was thoroughly confused. "Sorry?"

Neja growled, grabbed me by the ears and pulled me down to kiss her. Soundly.

Now, I'd kissed Neja before, at the meet and greet for the rock troll coronation. That was enough to make me a bit incoherent, but it was ultimately a display of power on Neja's part. She'd been, in some small way, putting her claim on me as the most powerful beings in the room. She'd known that my Reaper abilities put me in a class above most of the attendees, and kissing me without recrimination or protestation was her way of raising her own status. That, and I think she'd actually wanted to do it. But between the public display and the aftermath of my time with the rock trolls, I hadn't taken it as anything serious.

This, though, was entirely different.

For one, there was fire. Literally. It sparked around us, forming from the embers that floated around Neja's hair and burned in her eyes. I could feel the heat, the energy, but I didn't hurt and I didn't burn. Where our skin touched, the embers turned into pure electricity, shocking through me and making my hair stand on end.

I grabbed her waist with my right hand and tugged her close. Neja made a pleased noise and I kissed her harder. It was, to be honest, the most erotic thing I'd ever done, kissing her in the middle of a circle of fire, my two hearts beating impossibly fast and sending blood to the tips of my fingers and every spot where Neja touched me, as well as other more important places.

Neja pulled back abruptly. The flames flickered out. I gasped for breath and nearly staggered back a step. I gaped at Neja and she just smirked. "Do you understand, now?"

I nodded vaguely. "I think so."

"Good. We can work on better explanations later. Without an audience."

Neja reached up and smoothed out my hair, then threaded her arm through my numb left arm. She turned to look at Calvin and Sebastian, who were both staring openly. Her brows quirked upwards. "Yes?" she asked cooly. "Do you need something?"

"Um," Sebastian managed.

"No, we're good!" Calvin squeaked.

I felt flushed. Not knowing if this was a good thing, I shoved the feeling down and turned to Agravane. My voice came out a bit squeaky, so I cleared my throat. "H-how—how do we find Fate if Death's heart is, er, unavailable?"

Agravane blinked for a moment. He looked between Neja and myself, shook his head, then repeated the motion. "Right. Sorry. Just distracted. Fate. Right."

"Breathe, Agravane," Neja said.

The aurai did as she commanded, taking a few deep breaths then giving us a weak grin. "Okay, Fate. Well, last time, we came here on the advice of that warrior or whoever. He directed us, we came. Death's heart didn't really react until, what, the manticore attacked you, was what you said?"

Sebastian nodded. "Indeed. Fate appeared directly afterwards."

"We could wander around this place until she appears again," Calvin suggested.

"I doubt that Fate is going to do the same thing twice," Agravane replied. "From what you described, she's a bit on the unpredictable side."

"Unstable would be more like it," Sebastian muttered. I pretended not to hear him, and so did everyone else, just in case she was listening. I didn't need Death's mother appearing just as we were complaining about her.

"Can you use Death's heart to find her, even if it's, ah, you know?" Agravane asked, pointing at my chest.

I shook my head. "I don't think so. All it seems to do is give me the ability to take life."

That was putting it mildly, but I didn't have the words to describe what it was like with that feeling of life in the darkness, that unreachable high when I took the lifeforce of a being. There were depths of that power I was sure I had yet to plumb, but I couldn't quite bring myself to explore it, even in theory.

"Then we'll have to find her another way. What if we go somewhere she's likely to be?" Calvin asked. "Like how you find Life at a party and Death at a funeral, things like that?"

"Where would you even find Fate?" Neja drew her brows together. She looked at me. "I mean, I would have thought she'd be following you around like a lost puppy the way you seem to cause trouble, but she's not here, now is she?"

"Do you think she was the one who orchestrated the mix-up about working for Death?" Sebastian asked. He looked at Calvin. "You never did tell us what had caused the mistake, only that it was a mistake."

Neja looked up at me in question.

"Remember that note from Croatia several centuries back? The one in my handwriting that said 'the employment was a mistake'?"

Neja scoffed. "Of course I do. You've been ignoring it for a year, at least."

I cringed, but she wasn't wrong. "Well, Calvin wrote it. Death apparently hadn't meant to hire me. I was the wrong person. It was an accident." Saying it out loud didn't make it any more real to me than it had been when Calvin brought it up the first time. Of course, I'd been furious at my soul and hadn't really considered the fact since. Now, though, I thought about it and still didn't really believe it. I was a Reaper, a marketing agent, a descendent of Knights. How could Death have made a mistake in hiring me?

"Whatever Cal's job situation, which is a problem we can sort out *later*, thank you, I don't think Fate is hanging around right now," Agravane said. He looked around at the henge and the trees beyond it, all silent and empty. "We need to go somewhere else."

Where would you even find Fate in a natural setting? Calvin had been right; you could find Life at just about any party. Death did tend to show up at funerals. But Fate?

"I've got it," I said. Then I winced and hoped I was right. "But it's not going to be particularly pleasant."

"Where, Cal?" Neja asked. "Surely we can handle it."

I muttered the answer under my breath. Maybe I was wrong. Maybe she would just appear in the next three seconds and I would never have to relive some of the most awkward minutes of my entire life.

"Louder, Cal," Agravane said with a sigh. "It can't be that bad."

I winced. It could, actually.

"Speed dating," I said. "A speed dating event. Or one of those singles mixers."

Four sets of eyes stared at me. I fiddled with the numb fingers of my left hand, wondering if maybe massage would get the blood flowing again. No such luck.

The eyes kept staring.

Silence weighed down on me, pressing from all angles until it was hard to breathe. "Those stupid dating events where you go into a room with a whole bunch of other people and either spend three minutes talking to one person before moving on or just wait until a pretty girl lets you buy her a drink, then everyone starts pairing off and talking about how it's fate that brought them there and why can't all dating be this easy, but you're the only one who can't get one of the other people to actually spend more than five minutes talking with you because your cousin keeps texting and interrupting, and all the conversation starters you prepared are completely irrelevant and no one wants to talk about a marketing job at a speed dating event, so you're stuck trying to make small talk about the weather and giving complements and it's truly awful."

I sucked in a breath. "I hadn't meant to say all that."

"So I gathered," Sebastian said, hiding a grin behind his hand.

"Do you know, I had forgotten about that night?" Calvin scratched his beard. "That really was awful. And wasn't it a favour for Baz, because he had promised to be a test subject for this new algorithm they were using, only he'd started seeing someone the night before?"

"They broke up two weeks later," Sebastian agreed, his grin widening. "Those researchers had a field day with you! They were flummoxed about your inability to hold normal conversation. Didn't they end up writing a research paper on you?"

"Yes, yes, moving on," I complained. "If there's anywhere Fate might be, it's going to be at one of those things. I've never heard people invoke Fate more frequently than during dating and romance and whatnot."

Neja snickered. "I would have loved to see you at one of those events."

"No," I said, shoving my glasses up my nose. "You wouldn't. It's worse than karaoke. Much worse. Now, is there something like that in the Goblin Market?"

"Oh yes," Agravane said with a feral look. "I know just the place."

CHAPTER 16

"For someone who doesn't spend much time in the Goblin Market, you really do have an uncanny ability to navigate," Sebastian said as Agravane led us up the steps of what looked, in all honesty, like a replica of Versailles cut into the wall of the Market. It had hedges and flowers and fountains out front, and the facade of the building, while cut into cave stone, gave one the sense of being in France. It was one of the stranger things I'd seen in the Market.

"I heard about this place from a friend of a friend," Agravane said with a casual shrug. "He said it was the best place to hold events, that there are loads of things going on at one time. Food tastings, concerts, magic conferences, speed dating, everything."

"Great," I muttered. The closer I stepped to the palace, the more I could feel my skin itching. It was an allergic reaction, surely. I was allergic to speed dating and singles mixers. It just wasn't possible for me to enter without breaking into hives. I should just go home now and wait for the reaction to pass.

"Cal, breathe," Neja said, patting me on the back with more force than was necessary. I stumbled up the steps. "You're not actually here for the event, you're just waiting for Fate."

"Hi! Are you here for the event?" A chipper woman with bright green skin and iridescent wings, her hair a dandelion yellow, fluttered over to the five of us. A pixie, and an annoyingly cheerful one at that.

Before I could stop him, Agravane fixed her with a wide grin. "Yes, yes we are!"

As one, Calvin, Sebastian, and I huffed and grumbled. Neja coughed a laugh into her hands. The pixie didn't look at all perturbed, just flashed a bright smile and waved us onwards. Without looking back to check if we were following, or paying attention, she launched into a speech that was obviously well-rehearsed and terrifying.

"These days, it's so hard to find real romance in the world. You have so many realms out there, and your soul mate could exist on any one of them. But finding them is nearly impossible, because you're inundated with all this nonsense, all this content, that is designed to draw your attention to it. You interact with hundreds of people a day, but the interactions aren't meaningful. They're empty, meant for the consumption of the masses, which leaves you feeling lonely in a world full of lonely people. That's where we come in, the Lonely Hearts Club, meant to help all those people looking for true and real connection to come together in such a way that makes romance possible again. It crosses realms, it defies boundaries, it's like fate is just trying to bring you together. So, what are your names and what are you looking for in your love connection?"

I hadn't realised that the pontificating had come to an end and just kept nodding. The pixie turned to look at us and I stiffened. Tried to smile. Decided better of it.

"Um, er," said Calvin. He looked at me with wide eyes full of panic, and I couldn't blame him. Even insane, he could obviously tell this was a bad idea.

"Great choice!" the pixie said after a moment of silence, somehow still genuinely cheerful despite her audience. "Letting the universe decide for you. It's such an underrated experience. Now, come this way and I'll take you to the first ballroom, where you'll be started off in our speed dating trials."

"Trials?" Sebastian asked, sounding suspicious.

"Drinks, of course!" the pixie giggled. I wondered how quickly I could find an exit in this maze of a palace. Even the loo would be better than this. Drinks? I shuddered.

Agravane nudged me in the side with the pointy end of his elbow before I could say something snarky, like announcing the fact that I couldn't get drunk. I wondered if my soul could. It made sense; he'd got all my emotion, why wouldn't he also get my ability to drink and actually enjoy it?

That thought was almost more depressing than speed dating.

The ballroom was, as one would expect, stupidly

grand. There were floor to ceiling windows, which made no sense as the palace was recessed into a cave wall, curtains of some vibrant silk brocade fabric, marble floor tiles in a pattern that would have taken ages to make, and more. Everywhere I looked there was gilt and glitter, signs of opulent wealth and over the top facade. It was, frankly, a bit nauseating.

In the middle of the ballroom, taking up only a tiny portion of the room, were several tables. They were small, with a chair on either side, covered in a white tablecloth and lit with a candle. The lighting around the tables was suitably dramatic and moody, making it just hard enough to see the people already there that I had to squint.

The people waiting were from a wide variety of species, with a wide variety of looks. None of them, though, were of the sort that was well-kempt, confident, or in any way intimidating. I would hazard a guess that they were on the lower end of the power spectrum in Elsewhere, and they were here because it was neutral, safe, and provided a way to meet others that would not normally be provided to them.

I felt a bit bad for them, using their desperation like this, so that I could summon Fate. Then I remembered the fact that my left arm was hanging limply at my side and I didn't feel so bad anymore. They would find someone at another event. Surely.

The hyper-positive pixie ushered us to our chairs without any delay, clapping her hands as we sat. Then, with a deep inhalation, she chirped, "Begin!" and horrible things began to happen.

The person I was to speed date first introduced herself as Marcie. She was, I believed, some sort of golem or gargoyle or something. Her skin looked like limestone, and her eyes were some sort of purple crystal that flashed when she spoke.

"What do you do for a living?" she asked. I sighed. Why couldn't people ask more interesting questions when trying to get to know someone?

"I do marketing."

Marcie tilted her head, crystalline eyes blinking brightly. "You run markets? Like for vegetables and livestock?"

"Er, not quite. It's all about selling things to people in a way that increases sales and interest in large quantities. Adverts. Graphics. Campaigns. That sort of thing." I could tell it was going well when Marcie did that strange blinking thing again. I took a hasty sip of the drink that was on the table—some sickly sweet port —and winced. "What about you, Marcie, what do you do?"

She tossed her head. "I am a model."

"Oh? That's cool. Do you do photoshoots or paintings or…?" I took another sip of the bad port.

"I stand still while wearing expensive jewellery, and then people buy it. I am very good at standing still. It's genetic." Marcie tossed her head again and I'm fairly certain that the lights in her eyes winked at me. I tried to come up with something to say, anything at all, but my words failed me. What does one say to a living rock who models dead rocks? How ironic? I didn't think that would go over well.

"Lovely weather we've been having," I blurted out. Marcie frowned.

"You are a terrible conversationalist," she announced just as the tiny bell that indicated a switch in partners rang. Without a backwards glance, she stood and flounced off to the next table. The next candidate was a form that appeared genderless, made up of mostly leaves. It tittered at me as it sat.

"Did you know that there's an *aurai* here?" they asked, voice high and excited. I looked over its shoulder to the table beyond and found Agravane actually leaning away from the person at his table. He looked severely disturbed. "They're all so beautiful, don't you think?"

"Er, yes," I said. "So, I'm Cal. What's your name?"

The creature responded with a series of sounds like the wind through trees that I couldn't possibly replicate if I tried. I nodded, smiled as best I could, and sipped more at my port.

"So, who are your patrons in Elsewhere?" the creature asked. "Everyone here has patrons that are trying to match them up and secure their future. That's what this event specialises in. Isn't that great?"

My smile felt brittle. "Yes, great. Who are your patrons?"

The creature let off another set of noises, this time like water over rocks, and I nodded as seriously as I could. They launched into a story about their patrons and their exceeding kindness towards them, which thankfully kept me from having to talk about Death and Life, or the weather.

This went on for almost an hour, the incessant small talk making me want to tear out my hair. After dealing with forgotten gods and furious witches and Fate herself, I should have been better able to handle this sort of event, but I couldn't even bring myself to smile during most of it. The conversations were truncated and unhelpful, and the drinks were bad. What was it with the Goblin Market and bad drinks?

Finally, the pixie released us from the torture of the short conversations to a more open mixing around the room. Several people gravitated towards Agravane and his charming smile and annoyingly good looks. A few others found Neja and nodded their heads over what looked to be a serious conversation. Calvin and Sebastian wandered over to me.

"This is a waste of time," Sebastian growled. "She's not coming."

"She'll be here," Calvin said, but as with most things, there was a note of desperate uncertainty in his voice. "She has to be here."

Honestly, I was out of ideas. If Fate didn't show at this ridiculous event, then I would have to come up with other means of hunting her down. There was no way that I was going to parade all over Elsewhere and the mortal realms, attending dating events and hoping that she appeared at one of them. I couldn't think of anywhere else she might frequent, and pinning down someone so powerful as Death's mother was not going to be easy without a plan. And this one was moments away from failing.

Agravane laughed, the sound cheerful and happy. At least one of us was enjoying ourselves.

Then, movement in the room seemed to slow. The liquid in people's drinks defied gravity for one brief instant before floating gently back into their glasses. The lights flickered. I could feel every muscle in my body—minus my left hand—begin to tighten in anticipation.

"Hello, Godkiller."

I turned and found Fate leaning against the bar, her hair floating gently around her, as if she weren't dangerous, as if she were merely beautiful. She held out a glass with amber liquid in it and I took it, sipping carefully in case it was something really bad. It was nothing more than a whiskey, well-aged and full of peat flavour.

"Did you know that would happen?" I asked. "That I would be forced to kill the Elderkin?"

Fate chuckled. "Forced? Oh, no, dear Cal. No one forced you."

"Didn't they?" I tilted my head. "I offered them a choice. And a choice offered by a Reaper comes to pass, one way or another. Or have I mistaken the way of things?"

Her jaw tightened a touch, just enough to show frustration. Then, she smiled again. "Perhaps. Though there were a great many choices you could have offered. Killing them was up to you."

"Stop prevaricating," Sebastian said, stepping closer. I handed him the whiskey and he drank, nodding appreciatively. "You manipulated events to put us in the situation where killing the Elderkin was the most likely option. You knew how they would react to a potential threat, you knew how we would react to any hint of danger towards our friends. Put the right players on the board at the right time and the conclusion is, shall we say, foregone?"

Fate turned to Calvin. To my surprise, he stared her down, no hint of discomfort in his features. He stood straight and tall and with all the appearance of capability. There was even an emotion in his eyes that I would be hesitant to name as anything other than righteous fury.

"And what of you, wandering soul?" Fate purred. "Do you think I manipulated things?"

"When haven't you?" Calvin replied in much the same tone. He gave a dark smile. "You are Fate, after all, or a being close enough that the semantics make no difference. You weave the currents of the universe into patterns that please you. You are not as inevitable as your son, for people can rail against you and deny their natures, but who among us is really strong enough for that?"

Fate reached behind the bar and grabbed another glass, topping it with whiskey. "For that speech, you deserve a drink."

"I will drink nothing from you, witch," Calvin snarled. "You ruined my life. And you will continue to ruin it, or am I mistaken in your interest with us?"

"Calvin?" I asked, a little uncertain. My soul shook his head at me.

"Don't you understand? She orchestrated the

circumstances of our employment," Calvin said, pointing an accusing finger at Fate. He was crying now, his anger spilling out in salty tears. "She pushed us into the exact situation where I would be lost to history, where you and Sebastian would be made, where we would be here, Godkillers, Reapers, insane, ready for whatever task she has for us."

As one, we looked at Fate. She seemed completely unconcerned by the scrutiny, busying herself with mixing a drink. The nebula pattern on her skin swirled slightly and her hair became a little more agitated in its movement, but otherwise she was the picture of calm.

"What task, exactly, did you have in mind?" Sebastian asked.

Fate shrugged a single shoulder, her smile dangerous, deadly. "Really, dear men, what else would you expect? That you are not here for some purpose? The magic of Elsewhere can function on coincidence, but things run so much more smoothly when there are… suggestions as to how things should go. It keeps everyone in line. It keeps history from remembering this point as the point where the realms imploded due to some foolish mistake."

"So, what, you take away free will?" Calvin demanded. His voice was shrill, but not quite close enough to yelling to gather notice from the people still going through the speed dating circuit. Agravane and Neja were still wrapped up in their conversations, not even looking in our direction.

No, that wasn't right. They couldn't see us at all, their attention so engrossed that we were invisible.

Not one person looked our way, even for an instant. We were invisible. Or they didn't know we were missing. That would mean Fate had something to hide.

Death's heart thumped strongly against my ribcage, and I knew I was right.

"Never," Fate insisted. "I merely suggest. I move pieces around with whispers, offers, options. I persuade. I hint. I prod. The choices a person makes are theirs alone, even if I do often know them better than they know themselves. After all, how else could I get people to do what I want, even when it's truly terrible?"

"What task do you have for us? For me?" I asked. Sebastian and Calvin stood at my shoulders, a united front against Fate. For the first time since meeting her, she faltered. There was uncertainty in her gaze and her fingers tightened around her glass enough to make it wobble, though it didn't crack.

She smiled again, as smooth and charming as ever. "My, my, what a stubborn streak you have, Calvin Montgomery Thorpe."

"Is the use of my full name meant to scare me?" I raised my brows. Lots of people knew my name. It wasn't some great secret.

Fate sighed. "I know a great deal more about you than your name. I know that neither of the two hearts in your chest can be removed. I know that you still fade while you are in separate bodies from your soul. I know that there are changes coming which no realm could foresee. And you are at the centre of them, whether you like it or not."

"Is that meant to scare us?" Sebastian growled. "We want no part in your games."

"I'm afraid it's too late for that." Fate reached out and tapped me in the chest. "Once you took the heart of Death into your body, you set into motion a game that has been millennia in the making. The power balance of the world has shifted, Cal, and it is your doing."

I knew, instinctively, that she was right. I also knew that whatever this change was, it couldn't be good. I had no intention of playing her games, though.

"Put us back together," Calvin said, breaking into my thoughts. I started, flinching into Sebastian, who rolled his eyes and ignored me.

"What?" Fate asked, frowning.

"Put Cal and Sebastian and me back together. Into one body. One person." Calvin threw his shoulders back and lifted his chin. He did not look at me.

Fate laughed, the sound ricocheting off the walls of the palace. As one, the people in the ballroom froze in place, eyes wide. The curtains moved as if with some impossible breeze. The floor cracked where Fate stood, her power leaking out of her with that one simple sound.

She fixed Calvin in her gaze, wearing a fox's grin. "It doesn't really fit with my plans."

Silence descended. We stared at her. After a moment, Fate's smile widened.

"You don't understand?" she crooned. "I said, no."

CHAPTER 17

I don't generally like to think of myself as petulant or needy. I was a fairly self-sufficient child, living in a home with a single mother who was extremely loving but with the exterior of an emotionless, superbly well-dressed statue. Between that, and taking care of my wayward cousin Baz, circumstances led me to be generally able to fend for myself. I rarely put up a fight when people told me no, either giving up on whatever it was or figuring out a way to get it myself.

But when Fate stood there and *laughed* at me, refusing to put me back together, when she'd been the ultimate cause of tearing me apart, I will admit to throwing a bit of a tantrum. Actually, all three of me threw tantrums.

It was, as you might imagine, somewhat more dramatic than necessary.

Sebastian exploded into the eldritch being of nightmares that was the full Reaper form, full of coils and fangs and shadows. I dived into the depths of that vast galaxy of emptiness and stars and desperate longing. And Calvin? He who had no power except what remained of his shattered mind? He lunged forwards before Fate could retaliate and wrapped his hands around her throat.

The entire world seemed to still. The cracks that Fate had caused in the floor spread no further. The curtains no longer moved with that impossible breeze. The people who had finally taken notice of us stood there as if their breaths were held, their muscles impossibly frozen. All the ambient energy that told of a world in motion just stopped.

Fate sucked in a shaky breath, her eyes fixed on Calvin. She blinked, and the world fell away. It reappeared a moment later in a lattice of trees and quiet, familiar and emptier than it should have been. We were back in the forest of heroes, no longer anything but an empty forest in the far reaches of the Goblin Market now that the gods who kept it were dead. I was really done with this place.

The trees still glowed with quiet light. Sebastian and I were still in whatever throes of shadows and death that had overtaken us. Calvin still stood with his hands wrapped around Fate's throat. But the feeling of things had changed. Momentously.

The trees leaned away from us, their roots groaning as they tried to make their swift escape, though they were too mired in the ground to make it far. What little undergrowth there was curled and withered in a wide circle around us. Even the rocks tried to flee, rolling away. Only one remained unmoving, unafraid of what was going on, and I realised a moment later that it was the corpse of the manticore, beyond caring about such things as souls and fate.

"Why bring us back here?" Sebastian demanded, twining his coils around the area of emptiness and looking down on us. He bared his impressive fangs, dripping with shadow. "Too afraid for anyone to see?"

Fate scoffed, though the sound was cut short by Calvin tightening his grip on her. "I brought us here because I am exceedingly fond of that palace, and all the events that it holds."

"I don't believe you," Calvin said. He pressed a thumb into the divot where her neck ended, and I could have sworn that I saw the nebula written on her skin flutter.

"Don't you know who I am?" Fate asked with a saccharine smile. "I am the Weaver of Worlds, the Oracle and the Prophet. I am the Binder, the Guiding Wind, the beginning of the end and the end of all things. I am Destiny and I am Fate and every thread in this universe will pass through my fingers to shape and to mould. I have existed long before you were even a thought on the wind, and I will exist long after you are nothing more than a forgotten memory like the gods you slew. What could I possibly have to fear from *you*?"

Calvin laughed, the sound broken and sharp. He squeezed a bit harder. Fate coughed, but she didn't fight back, she didn't push him off. She just stared, her eyes a little too wide for nonchalance.

"What do you have to fear from us? From me?"

Calvin parroted. He laughed again. "Lady, do you have any idea what I've been through? How little I have left to lose?"

I took a step forwards. The pulsating void that existed within me now spread out, touching each of us in turn. I saw the life of the trees, steady and strong, their minuscule and vast force little more than a quiet hum in the background of what stood before me. There was Sebastian, wreathed with gold and silver, impossibly alive. There was Calvin, full of jagged shards of immortality in vibrant shades of the same colours. Fate, a tapestry of almost pure gold, the vibration that her life gave off a call that drew me forwards, made me want to take that life into myself and see how it would taste. The temptation of the living for the dead, a dangerous siren's call, and one I was not inclined to refuse at that moment. I lifted my right hand, my left still limp at my side. The threads that wove through me were black and silver and gold, some sort of strangeness that I had never seen before.

Slowly, I lowered my hand. Fate's eyes tracked the movement, then flickered up to me in surprise. "A forgotten god asked me that not more than a few hours ago, and look how that turned out for her. I think that you, Fate, have a very *great* deal to fear from us," I said in a low voice. "You said yourself that people fight you. Even if they rarely succeed. You are not the inevitability of Death or the impossibility of Life. You can only whisper, weave, guide. And you've been guiding things for a very, very long time. Imagine, then, if we three were to oppose you at every step of the way? Imagine if we were to fight you? If we were to undo every weaving you've done so far, if we were to defy fate and destiny and everything else? What would happen, then?"

"You could not possibly do such a thing," Fate rasped. Her hair crackled with lightning.

"Couldn't I? After all, I am immortal. I can't die, no matter how often people try. And frankly, I don't do well with boredom. I have to have a purpose. I would happily pursue this goal. Every day. Until the end of time." I gestured to Calvin and Sebastian. "And I have no doubt that they would join in with me."

Fate's eyes flickered between us. Sebastian let out a growl that shook the earth. Calvin tightened his grip. I just waited.

"You will undo a great many plans if you are one instead of three," Fate said on a cough.

"I will undo a great many more if I am not put back together." I shrugged.

"What is so important that you wish to keep us apart?" Sebastian asked. His coils wrapped tighter around the four of us, even as the trees bent away further. "You said that the balance of the world is changing. How? To what end?"

Fate shook her head, her storm cloud hair floating around her face. "I cannot tell you," she said. Calvin growled, the sound almost more terrifying than Sebastian's equivalent noise. "Truly, I cannot say. I can weave the threads together, but only once the weaving is done will the picture become clear. It is why I can only nudge, suggest, not dictate and demand."

Calvin squeezed harder, and I could tell that he was starting to properly cut off her air. The golden threads that made up her being flared with light, desperate to get through. My soul was doing his best to kill her, and for all that she had done to him, I couldn't entirely blame him.

Still.

"Calvin, let her go," I said. He glared at me, but complied. Fate staggered back, rubbing at her neck. "Alright, then. If you cannot say what is coming, then how do you know things would be made so much worse by my being in pieces?"

She laughed, nothing so mocking as before. "Really, Cal. Are you so sure that logic will win out in this situation?"

I'd had that hope, I would freely admit that much.

"The world does not work that way, dear Cal. You may argue your way out of prosecution by the rock trolls, or through dangers posed by forgotten gods and old witches, but there are few things that are truly as rational as that."

Fate crossed her arms and began pacing. She drew closer to the edge of the clearing that had formed around us. Sebastian drew his coils back as she approached. Even the trees strained against their roots to pull away. Fate glared at them. Apparently Calvin was the only one crazy enough to touch her, and I wasn't certain that we wouldn't feel the repercussions later.

"The world doesn't make sense," she spat, waving her hands at the trees. "The trees pull away, though I have not personally done them harm. Your soul's mind has shattered, though many have endured as much as he has. You cannot impose order on a thing just because it makes you feel better. I don't know how I know that things will be made worse by your being split, I just do."

"Aren't you powerful enough to reweave whatever webs you've woven?" Sebastian asked. He gave a shake and those terrible coils and claws and fangs folded in on themselves until he was once more just a man, standing beside me, eyes dark and posture relaxed. Calvin whimpered, pressing his hands to his head. I couldn't help him through his insanity, not now, so I didn't, just pulling back on my own terrible power until I, too, was nothing more than a man. Exhausted and dirty, with a cracked pair of glasses, sure, but as human as I ever had been.

Fate watched this with interest. She sniffed and continued her pacing. "I can do a great many things, Reaper. I'm not sure reweaving your place in the world is one of them."

"You, who are the mother of Death? Who are so powerful that you hold the threads of every life in your grasp?" Sebastian scoffed. Somehow, I didn't think that was a good thing. "No wonder you fear being opposed."

Fate took in a deep breath in. Around her, the trees strained as if they were being pulled in and wanted desperately to escape. I saw leaves fall towards her, brushed away by a careless hand. She huffed and shook her head. The trees relaxed. "You don't understand such things. How could you? For all that you hold the power to shake the world in your hands, you are nothing more than human. Dangerous, unstable, human."

Fate straightened and smiled benevolently. "Very well, Calvin Montgomery Thorpe. I will give you the means to put yourself back together. But how you fit the pieces is up to you. Will your soul remain the sentient being? Or your Reaper abilities? Or will the pieces in between? Each a fully formed mind, each capable of so very much."

She held out a hand, something shining there. A dagger, gleaming and silver, what looked like an opal set into the hilt. It was thin, like a stiletto, but ornate. "In order to be whole again, you must slay those pieces of you which remain free."

Before I had a chance to process those words, figure out just what they meant and how I was actually meant to go about doing something productive with them, Calvin lunged for the knife in Fate's hands.

Of course he did.

He leaped for Sebastian first, all those centuries of training finally coming in handy. He might have been crazy, but he wasn't incompetent. Sebastian hissed and pulled back, shadows covering every inch of his skin. Instead of forming again as the nightmare being that he could be, he just remained dark and terrible. Claws tipped his fingers and the beginnings of horns sprouted from his brow.

Calvin didn't seem at all bothered. He just kept dancing forwards, the dagger held with expert ease, his steps even and steady. "Why do you resist?" he demanded. "Isn't this what you wanted?"

"Cal is the host, not you," Sebastian snapped. That response cost him, though. Calvin managed to slice Sebastian on the forearm, shadows leaking out of the wound like blood. Instead of healing, as the various wounds we inflicted on each other had done previously, the shadows kept flowing.

That dagger could do exactly what Fate suggested. Kill us.

"Sebastian, run!" I ordered. It didn't work, not that I really expected it would. My Reaper abilities were as much me as was Calvin. That is, stubborn and persistent.

Calvin ducked under a fist and cackled as he leaped. Sebastian managed to block another cut with the meat of his arm, but though his claws dug into Calvin's skin, eliciting screams of pain, the wounds didn't last. Only the dagger could hurt us permanently.

"I don't want to remember," Calvin laughed, the sound halfway to a sob. "But I can't forget, either."

"There is no need for you to forget," Sebastian said, trying to reason with my soul. Calvin was not to be reasoned with, however.

All of this only took a few seconds. I barely managed to gather my senses enough to take a step forwards, ready to step in, when Calvin's superior training and plain unpredictability won the day. He plunged the dagger right into the centre of Sebastian's chest. The Reaper grunted and stiffened, staggering back, the knife embedded in his chest as his muscles closed around the blade. He let out a hiss of air and fell, staring at me in shock.

Then, the shadows flowed forwards into Calvin, like some great vacuum hoovering up magic. The dagger fell to the ground.

I'd like to say I leaped for it before Calvin could recover, before he could do more damage and try to kill me. I'd like to say that I quietly and quickly pulled both him and Sebastian into me, making myself whole once again. I'd like to say that very much.

The truth is that I was too slow.

Calvin and I leaped for the dagger at the same moment. His hand grabbed the hilt. Mine grabbed the blade.

I'll give you one guess which hurt more.

CHAPTER 18

I flinched back from the blade, taking several steps away from Calvin while I mentally cursed myself. I was already working with only one arm, the left one being completely useless. I didn't need to take myself completely out of the fight. My palm dripped blood, but the pain receded after a few seconds. That probably wasn't a good thing, as it likely meant the wound was more serious than I thought, but I accepted it.

Calvin flew at me with eyes wide and glasses askew. The knife gleamed in the half-light of the forest. I dodged. Poorly. The very tip of the blade grazed my left shoulder, another wound I couldn't feel. So far, this fight wasn't going well for me.

I couldn't beat Calvin in a straight up knife fight. Sebastian had shown me that much, though it had likely cost him a great deal. Calvin had too many centuries of fending off people who were interested in the raw power he exuded as pure soul. And I'd proven to be totally useless in a fight.

To be fair, this was just about the first time since coming to work for Death that I'd actually feared the outcome of a fight. It was amazing how overconfident you could be when dying was off the table.

I didn't bother trying to remember the few moves that Agravane had taught me, instead relying entirely on instinct. Calvin lunged and swung wildly, doing his best to get at me with the knife in any fatal way. My neck, my heart, my lungs, anything vital would seem to do. He kept lunging, parrying, hacking. I kept retreating.

I felt a tree at my back and spun aside just as Calvin stabbed with an overarm swing. The dagger lodged itself into the bark of the tree. Calvin struggled for a moment, trying to pull it out. I took my chance, dropping low and tackling him to the ground.

It felt a bit like brawling with Baz when we were boys, each of us trying to get the upper hand. I usually managed to outsmart Baz in a fight, but he was more skilled. This time, I tried to do as he would have and knocked the glasses clean off Calvin. It wouldn't make him blind, as my vision was bad, but not so bad as to make the world a complete blur. Smearing the blood of my hand onto his eyes, though, would make the world a blur.

He snarled and reached for me, scratching at my chin. I managed a punch to his jaw. He yelped, his struggles relaxing for a moment. I scrabbled off of him, going for the tree and the knife. With two good yanks,

I pulled the weapon from the tree. Calvin then tackled me from behind.

"I won't let you do this!" he screamed, knocking me to the ground hard enough that the dagger flew from my grasp. "I won't!"

"Why not?" I huffed, reaching for the knife while he tried to hold me back. "I've already seen everything about your life. I know what happened to you. I'm not likely to forget any time soon."

"You don't understand," Calvin said. He let go of my sweater long enough to scramble forwards and try for the knife. I was just as fast, reaching for the thing just as he did. He had to stop to keep me from grabbing it, once again locking us into a struggle for control.

"Then explain it!"

Calvin shook me by the shoulders, his knee digging into my back. It knocked the air from my lungs, but didn't stop me reaching for the knife. "It wouldn't be the same. It wouldn't be me!"

With a heave of effort, I surged upwards, knocking Calvin off balance. He rolled, hand passing within inches of the knife. It was my turn to hold him down. I grabbed him by the collar, knocking his head into the ground twice so he would stop struggling. He just glared at me, tears clearing away some of my blood from his face.

"I *am* you," I growled. I shook him again. "I am *you*. You, me, Sebastian, we might be in separate bodies, have separate words, but we are all one and the same. If I remember what happened to you, it's because I am you."

Calvin kept crying, his body trembling. "It's not the same. It's not the same. It's not the same."

It was like a refrain, the way he kept mumbling the words, slurring them together. He was terrified of being absorbed back into me, despite being the one who had requested the action. He wanted this—or he knew that we needed this—but he couldn't bring himself to do it.

I got off of him, reaching for the knife. Calvin whimpered on the ground. I took the dagger and shoved it into my pocket, the closest thing to a sheath I had. Then I turned to Fate.

She was watching, enraptured. Her attention was fixed on us, her hands clasped together like she couldn't wait to see the outcome of the match. I curled my lip. "Do you enjoy this?" I demanded.

"Certainly," she replied. "But why did you stop? This could all be over now if you—"

"This is sick. Some sort of sick game you delight in, pitting me against myself, just to see which part of me will win out. Do you enjoy torturing people? Taunting them? Seeing how they will accept their fate or fight it?" I took a step closer. Maybe the dagger would be just as effective against her, though I doubted it. Still, it might feel good to stab her, even if just in the shoulder.

"Do you know why I am more feared than Death? More powerful than Life?" Fate asked with a twisted smile. She held out her hands and a stream of glowing threads in all different colours filled the air. Most of the threads were short, dull, but a few stood out in both length and brightness. "Life, beloved of all, unpredictable and loveable, yet cruel and capricious in the same breath. Death, steady and immovable. Inevitable. Both pale in comparison to me, who weaves the future of the stars themselves. And yet, most never seek me out, never question my presence. Why? Because when I present them with their fate, it is often sad and lonely, short, useless. A single strand, meant to take up space or fulfil a singular purpose, such as setting someone else on a different path, being in the right place at the wrong time. It's necessary, Cal, for the creation of the future, that many must amount to nothing."

She took a step forwards. Her eyes gleamed with that void, hungry and keen. "But there are a few, like yourself, that *matter*. Whose threads can make up a whole section of tapestry. Who change the shape and colour of the world. They know that they are important to me, to Fate, and they accept it with pride. You, on the other hand, are so caught up in your own ridiculous self-righteous image that you can do nothing but resist me. Foolish. It will be pointless, in the end. But if I get to watch you destroy yourself, then I may as well take some enjoyment out of it."

I shook my head, disgusted. "You want to watch a soul broken into insanity fight me? Fight a creature of cold and logic and emptiness? You find Calvin's desperation entertaining? You find my reluctance to participate enjoyable? No wonder you're dangerous."

She said nothing, just smiled. And really, there was not much I could say that would change her mind. She was a force of the universe, as immutable as Death or

Life. She was herself, and trying to change that would be an impossible undertaking.

The only question was what to do now? As much as I didn't want to harm Calvin any more, I needed to get my soul back into my body. I was fading, as my left arm kept reminding me. And I would really, really rather not fade away. At the risk of damaging my own soul further, I would have to kill him. It was the only obvious way forward.

No sooner had I decided that, then I felt a sharp, burning pain in my back. I reached immediately for the knife in my pocket and found nothing. Staggering, I turned around. Calvin stood there, arms tucked around himself, weeping openly now. He didn't have the knife in his hand, but then, why would he? It was in my back, piercing my lungs and touching my heart.

I couldn't get any air. I tried, sucking in a breath only to find that my lungs were frozen and there was no air to be found. Black spots formed in my vision and I gave in to panic. I reached around and pulled out the knife in some feat of flexibility that I will likely never be able to reproduce. The blade was bloody, except for the tip. It was impossibly black, empty, like that void between stars. The one that existed in my chest.

I fell to my knees. My vision went nearly black before suddenly, I could breathe again. It wasn't quite right, like the air was being sucked out of the hole the knife had caused just as quickly as I could breathe it in, but I was breathing. My lungs began working, pulling in air in heavy gasps. I dropped the knife as I fought for breath. Calvin fell on his knees before me.

"No, no, no," he said, reaching out and patting at my sweater, like he was checking me over for injuries. "No, no. You're not…I didn't…not like this…I don't—"

"I'm alright," I reassured him on a rasp, though I don't know why. I heaved in another breath. "You pierced my lungs and hit Death's heart. Not mine. You didn't kill me. It's okay. You're not a killer."

Though I didn't know how much longer I would stay alive with the damage to my lungs. So much for fighting. Agravane was right; as soon as I was no longer immortal, I would be struck down. I just hadn't expected my soul to be the one to do it.

"But your lungs!" Calvin cried. He shook his head, whimpering.

"Finish him off, little soul," Fate crooned. She appeared over his shoulder, her expression warm and pleasant. As I watched, my vision going spotty again, a bright thread floated from the tips of her fingers and started weaving itself around Calvin. I growled, reaching for her with what little strength I had left. Calvin started rocking in place, giving in to the meltdown.

"It's not…I don't…" he hiccoughed. I reached for the thread, trying to grab on to it. Fate just sneered at me and kept crooning at Calvin, using her persuasive magic to make him do what she wanted.

"It's cruel to make him suffer like this. The sooner he dies, the sooner you can be whole again. With you in charge, little soul. Your memories never forgotten. Ever."

Fate brushed her hand along Calvin's arm, that thread wrapping itself around him. I didn't think he could even see the thing, as he was so caught up in the horror of what was happening. Arm shaking, he reached for the knife I had dropped.

Then, a flash of blue. *No*, I thought, a hint of desperation starting to colour my thoughts. *Not again.*

Tempest appeared, her feathers out of their neat placement. Her wings were spread wide and her fur stood up on end. She looked harried, like she'd searched the whole of the Goblin Market for me. And, just as she had done before she died, she stood between me and danger. She tried to fix my mistakes.

Fate curled her lip at Tempest. "Get out of here, griffin. You're dead and have no place here. Not anymore."

Tempest beat her wings and screamed at Fate, the tiny creature standing up to something potentially more than a god. I reached for her, my breath even more ragged than before. Calvin could kill me, I didn't care, so long as Tempest was safe.

So long as…

I was out of time…

No more air…

Just—

I heard a scream of fury and a gasp of pain in the same instant. Almost immediately, my lungs became whole again and my vision became clear. Energy rushed through my limbs, making my entire body tingle. I flexed the fingers on both hands and held them up, watching as the various wounds I'd been dealt over the last few days all healed, leaving nothing behind but clean skin. I felt the Reaper abilities that had been suppressed while Sebastian was separate from me roar into existence again, a thousand shadows splintering beneath my skin, mine to command as I wished. I felt emotions begin to stir, stronger than I'd felt for what felt like centuries.

Too late, I realised what had happened.

Before me, curled over himself, Calvin began to fade, flowing into me. He smiled, the last expression I saw before he dissipated entirely and left behind nothing more than the knife he'd thrust into his own heart. My soul had killed himself to save me.

And he'd done it against the urging of Fate.

Tempest let out another scream, then launched herself into the air, flying straight through Fate and to the trees on the far side of the clearing. I took in several deep breaths, the changes taking place now that I was whole again too rapid for me to follow. What I could follow was the way Fate's eyes widened, her horror open and vivid.

"He shouldn't have done that," Fate whispered.

I didn't bother answering her. Instead, I stood, strength surging through my blood. I called up every shadow and scrap of Reaper power. I dived deep into the abyss of Death's heart. I let the fury and wrath and sorrow and pain of my soul flow freely. Then, I reached for Fate.

Fate recoiled, hands coming up to protect her face. I

grabbed a wrist and turned, some instinctive thing in me—a memory from Calvin, perhaps—having me turn so that I pulled her over my hip. My shadows leaped for her and wrapped around her skin, binding her hands together. She struggled, those terrible threads of hers surging forth and tangling with my shadows and void.

I growled, reaching for her again. My skin became night and the world leeched itself of colour except those few traces of lifeforce that Fate and the trees and I shared. When I grabbed her neck, it wasn't a hand that wrapped around her throat, it was a taloned foot. And when I screamed at her, it was a roar that escaped my throat.

I wrapped my coils around themselves, shadows dancing in the air between me and her. Fate struggled under my grasp, wrapping her threads around me. I twisted and broke them, the feeling like throwing off chains, no longer bound by someone else's direction. Fate's eyes went wide and her mouth fell open. Then, she began struggling in true desperation.

Her hands clawed at me, nails biting into the shadows that made up my flesh. I let out a hissing laugh. "Do you honestly think that you can do me harm, now that I've chosen to throw you off, to do things *my* way?"

Fate didn't reply, bucking and screaming under my weight. I didn't know what other powers she might have, whether she could call someone to her or not. I decided not to wait around and find out, instead picking her up in my claws and leaping through the forest. The trees bent out of my way, the ground blurred beneath my movements. This place feared us, Fate and me. I couldn't bring myself to care just then.

Finally, I broke through the forest and stopped. I dropped Fate to the ground and pulled the nightmare that was my Reaper manifestation back inside my skin. I brushed off my sleeves and smiled at Fate as she pushed herself off the ground and glared at me.

"Do you recognise where we are?" I asked.

Fate turned to look. Everything about her went still, from the nebulas painting her skin to the storm in her hair. "Why have you brought me here?" Fate breathed.

The crystal henge began to glow gently, a sight almost mesmerically beautiful in the midst of the darkness of the forest. It was entrancing, this thing that the dead gods had used to protect themselves, to keep themselves here in this place of forgotten heroes.

"Don't you know?" I asked, adjusting my glasses. I was, I admit, being cruel, taunting her like this, but she had caused enough damage and had confessed to the intent of causing a great deal more. People were not playthings for her to pick up and discard when they became less useful. I'd had too many powerful beings do the same to me, and I was tired of it. She'd caused Calvin's death. She'd likely spun the threads that broke his mind. I could feel the edges of insanity pressing in on me, and I knew that more than Calvin's experiences had come with him when we were made whole again.

Fate stood, looking as regal as ever. She lifted her chin and looked down at me. "I am no fool, Cal."

"And yet you do not run?" I spread my hands in

supplication. "Surely, a being as powerful as you, as all encompassing as you, who bore Death and who writes the lives of the stars, could just disappear."

She winced, closing her eyes. Then opened them, gaze resentful. "I do not run."

"Or you cannot run," I suggested. "Bound up in your own fate? Caught in your own web? Because you know that it was always your fate to be bound, to be imprisoned so that the whispers you breathe into the minds of people who might otherwise choose differently are silenced? So that your threads cannot so easily wrap around the necks of the damned?"

Fate began to pace. It was slow, her movements elegant and calm, but she was like a tiger in a cage. "My influence on the world will not be gone."

"No, I doubt it is so easy to throw off the chains of fate." I took a step forwards, rolling up my sleeves. "But it will be far easier to choose our own future without you."

Fate swallowed nervously and took a step backwards. "There is another way," she whispered. "The threads here diverge. Another path. You could let me be free."

I chuckled, some fount of dark humour bubbling up, likely from the part of me that was Sebastian. "I think you and I both know which possibility is the more likely."

Fate looked like she wanted to argue, wanted to plead her case, wanted to attempt to flee, even. She put out her hands in a silent plea. The trees bent back from her, creaking in their desire to get away. The smaller plants curled up and withered. The henge glowed brighter.

"Please," Fate said. "What will my son say?"

"I have no idea." I shrugged. "But I'm sure I can explain it in a way he'll understand."

Threads exploded from her outstretched hands, reaching for me, one last attempt to try and throw me off, to give her a chance at escape. But she took a step back and tripped over something small, innocent. A hedgehog, sitting there frozen in fear. A simple creature in this forest of heroes, caused Fate to trip and fall directly into the henge. Her fate was sealed through the actions of one tiny hedgehog. I leaped forwards and slammed my hand on one of the monoliths of the henge, using the power of Death's heart to weave a void around the crystal. The giant stones shuddered and glowed, their power coming to life, their purpose turning inwards instead of outwards.

Instead of a place of protection, a last centre for the power of the gods I had killed, now this place was a prison for Fate, keeping her power contained. She stared at me from inside the henge, her arms wrapped around herself. "I'll escape one day, Cal," she breathed.

"I'm sure you will," I replied. "And I'll be waiting."

Then, I turned and walked away. After a few hundred metres, Tempest appeared, chirping as she landed on my shoulder and nibbled my ear. I flinched, then scratched under her chin. "Let's go get Neja and Agravane, Tempest. Then, we're going home."

Had this been me, before the reuniting with my soul, before I was pieced back together from broken parts, I probably would have felt nothing about trapping Fate. Perhaps I would have felt the idea of remorse, but no more. Now, I barely made it a few more steps before my legs gave out beneath me and I had to lean against a tree while I cried.

CHAPTER 19

With significant help from Tempest in regards to navigation, I made my way back through the Goblin Market to where Agravane and Neja waited outside that ridiculous palace. I didn't get many vendors calling out to me, trying to sell their wares. I managed to avoid any conversation with passers-by, too, desperate for whatever fix they sought. In fact, just about everybody left me alone.

I don't imagine I looked terribly friendly just then, with my clothing torn and my glasses cracked, covered in dirt and blood and tears and whatever else remained from my adventures. I also hadn't showered properly in what felt like a week. I was tired. I was hungry. My muscles ached and I was in a thoroughly foul mood.

In essence, I felt more human than I had in years, and with the power at my disposal, that was a dangerous thing. No wonder people stayed out of my way.

Agravane was the first to spot me, though it probably had to do with the glowing ghost of a griffin riding on my shoulder more than anything. He nudged Neja, who was sitting on the steps, twirling a knife and looking bored.

"Cal," Agravane said, smiling and very nearly bounding for me in what was perhaps the greatest display of enthusiasm I'd seen from him in a long time. "We thought you'd, well…not died, because you can't, but something terrible, probably."

"What happened?" Neja asked. She prodded at a gash on my shoulder and I winced. "Your arm isn't numb anymore."

Then, they both noticed the obvious and in turn took a tiny step back. Neja was the one who brought it up, her voice tight with a mix of uncertainty and interest. "There's only one of you."

I sat on the steps, groaning. I unlaced my shoes and pulled them off, dumping what felt like several hundred miles worth of dirt onto the ground. I'm sure the proprietors would get mad at me for it, but I couldn't find it in myself to care. Not about this. After a few minutes of sitting, I shrugged.

"I got Fate to put me back together," I said. I wanted to leave it at that, but Neja sat next to me and twined her fingers with mine. Those ridiculous tears pricked at my eyes again. I took a deep breath, trying to shove the emotion back. It worked. Somewhat.

"What happened, Cal?" Neja murmured.

"Fate showed up at the speed dating event, like I told you she would," I said. I scoffed. "I don't think anyone else even noticed."

"Not until the ground started to shake and there were several literal gods fighting right before us," Agravane said drily. "I assume that was Sebastian in the midst of all that draconic nightmare."

I nodded. "Sebastian was the nightmare. I was the void. Calvin was the only one smart enough to actually attack Fate. She whisked us away to the resting place of the doomed so we could have a little *chat* about the state of affairs. She refused to put me back together, we argued. Finally, she offered a fix, only I had to kill the others—or they would kill me—and whoever was left standing would be the final sentient mind, the others in the pieces that were torn off. Calvin…"

I clenched my fists, accidentally squeezing Neja's fingers too tightly. She hissed and I released her hand. "Sorry," I muttered, wiping tears from my eyes.

"Keep going," she said, instead wrapping her arm in mine. "What did Calvin do?"

"Killed Sebastian, tried to kill me, had one of his insane episodes and killed himself instead. Which leaves me. The last one standing, all my pieces and parts put back together again. Hurrah."

I decided not to tell them about what I'd done to Fate. During my time in Elsewhere, I'd discovered that the more power you displayed, especially over another being of great power, the more people feared you. Imprisoning Fate, mother of Death, would ensure that people would fear me, would quiver when I passed, and I was so tired of having that sort of power at my fingertips. I wanted to sleep for a week, maybe binge a streamed soap opera with Yolanda and Agravane, get caught up in my coffee.

I wanted to do marketing. I wanted to play games. I wanted to take a walk in the park. I didn't want to be whatever it was that I had become. At least, not right now. I was sure that the temptation of wielding that terrible power would pop up relatively soon, but for the moment, I wanted none of it.

"You have your soul again?" Neja asked, a bit breathless. I flicked my eyes to her and frowned. She was smiling? Didn't she understand what I'd just said. No, that was unfair. It was a good thing that I was pieced together again. She was just celebrating the victory.

"I have my soul again." I tried to smile, and for the first time in ages, it felt almost natural. Easy, even.

"With a look like that, we're going to have to redo all the employee pictures," Agravane said. "You surely can't keep a professional picture of you scowling if you can smile like *that*."

I glared at him.

"That's better. Grumpy Cal is still in there some-where." Agravane patted my head. Tempest nipped at his wrist. He yelped and drew back. "Is that griffin staying, then?"

"What griffin?" Neja asked.

Both Agravane and I gaped at her.

"Do you mean you can't actually see Tempest?" I asked. Neja frowned.

"The dead griffin? From the Great Northern Ridge?" She furrowed her brows, giving me that sympathetic look that one gives the potentially dotty. "She's dead, Cal."

"I am aware," I said. "She also happens to be a ghost sitting on my shoulder."

Tempest let out a chirp. She buried her head in my hair and purred, too, which was as endearing as it was frightening when paired with her claws kneading my shoulder.

"Er," was all Neja said.

"She's not connected with Death," Agravane said, snapping his fingers. "That must be it. None of the mortals we encountered could see her, and most of the others couldn't either. Only those of us with a connection to Death. You, me, the other yous, Fate."

"So…I have a pet ghost that only some people can see?" I asked. It seemed silly to grasp onto this topic just then, but after everything, I needed a little levity.

"Should be fun!" Agravane said. "Yolanda will have a field day!" He looked around. "As much as I'm all for taking a rest and such, especially after the disaster that was speed dating, can we at least do that somewhere with decent drinks? This place has not once served me a decent glass of wine."

Neja snorted. "I would have thought that all the attention of those females—and males, some of them— would have been enough to make up for the wine. You should have seen it, Cal. After you left, there was pandemonium. Half of the attendees threw themselves on Agravane, begging that he save them."

"Oh, and what about those that threw themselves

on you, begging for the same thing?" Agravane snapped.

Neja reached for a dagger in a blur of motion, grinning wickedly. "They quickly learned their lessons."

I snorted softly, shaking my head. It really was good to have these two back. I pushed myself off the steps and we started wending our way back through the Goblin Market. The journey this time through seemed to pass in a flash, and I would have even considered coming back for an afternoon out sometime in the very distant future.

I realised, a few minutes after stepping through the door that would lead us back to Austin, Texas, that I was happy. Actually, really, truly, mildly happy. A quiet feeling, given everything that my soul went through to give it to me, but a real one.

WALKING up the drive to the building where my office and flat was had the feeling of impending doom. I knew without asking that Yolanda had already gone home for the day. I also knew that my flat would not be empty when I arrived.

Agravane and I had dropped Neja off at her cottage with the promise of payment for her services within a few business days, and also that we would meet up for a date sometime in the next week. Then Agravane and I had turned towards the Lands of Silence and home.

"Why don't you head home?" I said, shoving my hands into my pockets. "It's late. Yolanda's probably gone already, and I think we both could use a couple days off."

Agravane eyed me warily. "Are you sure?" he asked. He felt that feeling of doom, too, then.

"Yes," I said. I wasn't at all sure. But nor did I think that Agravane had to be here for this.

"You'll call if you need me?" I knew he wasn't talking about work.

"I'll call," I said.

"Do you know, I think that might be the first time you've lied to me." Agravane looked at me. I looked away. "I'll be by in the morning, then. We can figure out all the ways that the return of your soul has changed things. Alright?"

I hesitated. Took a breath. Nodded.

"Right. Be seeing you then, Cal," Agravane said, and with a tiny wave, he was off the path towards his own house, further into the wilds of Death's estate.

I was left alone except for Tempest, who still rode my shoulder. She was enough of a comfort that it only took me a few seconds before I started forwards again. It was a foreign feeling to unlock my front door and climb the stairs to the second floor where I lived. Everything was the same, just as I had left it, but the sense of *home* was stronger than I'd ever known it.

As expected, the door to my flat was open.

"Cal." Death's voice was smooth, even, without a hint of anger or reprisal. I hunched my shoulders and stepped into the flat. Death was at my kitchen table, a tea service set before him, the pot still producing tea from its spout. "I made tea, if you would care to join me. Or perhaps you would prefer coffee?"

I sank into the chair opposite Death. "Tea is fine," I said, and meant it. Yes, I longed for coffee, but would be perfectly content with tea.

Death studied me for a moment. I studied him. He looked exactly as he had done, his dark suit contrasting with the impossible blackness of his skin. He wore a purple waistcoat and a matching pocket square in the suit jacket. His eyes held the voids of the universe that his mother had borne. I swallowed.

"I felt it, when it happened, you know," Death said in a low voice. I closed my eyes, on the verge of panic. "And I knew that it was theoretically possible, but there hasn't been a mortal in millennia that can hold that sort of power."

The edges of coherent thought were beginning to escape me. I could feel laughter bubbling up in my chest and I forced it down with a hasty drink of tea. I nearly spluttered; it was too sweet by far, enough to shock me out of hysteria.

"What are you going to do?" I asked in a whisper.

"There is nothing I can do," was the enigmatic reply. Was that because he couldn't free his mother since I had been the one to imprison her? Or was it that her fate had been woven into her life from the beginning by her own strange power, and even Death could not interfere?

"I'm sorry," I breathed, squeezing my eyes shut.

"Cal," Death said. I flinched, hunching my shoulders. "Cal, look at me."

I raised my eyes. He didn't look angry. He didn't even look mildly put out.

"You did what needed to be done. My heart was in danger of being absorbed by someone else, or worse, destroyed. That much power is volatile when let loose. I know that you did what you thought was right, in that moment. That taking my heart into your own body was the only solution. I cannot be angry when you were only protecting it, as I asked."

I gaped. I'd forgotten about his heart. I'd forgotten that I'd taken the very thing that had called Fate to me. A piece of his power, perhaps an impossibly large piece. I realised then that he wasn't talking about me imprisoning Fate. Maybe he didn't even know.

"I don't know what happens next," I admitted.

"The heart will slowly integrate into you. It has done so a fair amount already, from what I can tell, but in time it will be so completely a part of you that it is indistinguishable from your own organs. Though, I wouldn't recommend going to any doctors in the mortal realms. They can be a bit, how do you say, freaked out? When presented with evidence of things far beyond them." Death smiled. I couldn't stop gaping.

"But…but…your power!"

Death chuckled. "It's not mine anymore. Oh, yes, it has properties that mirror my own power, but you have made it yours. Do not fear, Cal, I have lived without a heart before, and I will do so again. The power I lost to you will replenish itself in time."

I took another desperate sip of tea. "How?"

It was a mistake as soon as I asked.

Death's eyes darkened and he tightened his grip on the cup. "Do you not feel that irresistible pull towards the lifeforce of those whose stars you see in that void?"

I nodded and studied the liquid in my cup. "What does that make me, now? It feels different from my Reaper abilities."

"It is. Similar, but separate. It is merely another talent you will have to exercise and practise." Death sighed. "Truly, I do not know what the future holds in store for you, Cal. In a very short amount of time, you have managed to make waves in the realms like never before. None of the previous Reapers had such, hmm, pernicious influence as do you. I do not know what it means. Neither does Life. Nor, I imagine, does my mother, though I suspect you know about that already."

He fixed me with a firm stare. I wilted. "You know what happened, then?" I asked in a dull voice. Of course he did. He was Death. How could he *not* know?

"The weavings of Fate have been strong for many generations. To have them suddenly go quieter, as though they were being suppressed? Yes, Cal, I know what happened." Death sighed. He poured himself another cup of tea, adding milk and sugar in precise movements practised over an endless existence. "Once again, you play with powers that ought to be beyond you. And I warn you, Fate will not remain imprisoned forever. Her whispers will still find those whose weavings would have been strong and vibrant. All you have done is suppress her power."

"Was it a mistake?" I asked, though I think I was asking this more of myself than anything.

"Not necessarily," Death replied. "I should perhaps be angry at you for trapping my mother, but as you know, that is a more human emotion than anything and I am far from human."

I tried to crack a smile at that and failed.

"You would not have done it if you did not feel it necessary. I know you well enough to believe that, no matter what you were feeling at the reuniting of your soul. But the fact remains, Cal, that in a few days you have done two things which will, I believe, shake the realms to their core. And I dearly hope you are up to facing the consequences."

Without touching his second cup of tea, Death rose, tugging at the cuffs on his sleeves as he watched me.

"Have I ruined things for you?" I asked, a more childish question than I'd thought possible after all I'd seen over the last few years.

Death merely tilted his head and smiled benignly. "My dear Cal, don't you know? I am Death. I will endure no matter what. I am inevitable, after all. Even for you."

The splints holding together whatever remained of my sanity after everything finally fell apart. I stared at Death for a moment. Then, I started laughing.

Oh, yes, the future would be interesting indeed.

THE END

ACKNOWLEDGMENTS

As always, I should like very much to thank you readers for sticking with me through this probably ridiculous, but oh so much fun series. I am grateful for each and every one of you!

A special thanks to Matt Schafer for the hedgehog idea. Honestly, it made the book.

Thanks also to Willow, for forcing me to get off my lazy bum and take her for a walk several times a day. This book would have been written much faster if you would just learn to be a dog who likes naps.

And thank you again, over and over to Fay Lane, the best cover designer I've met. This series has the best covers!

On, I think, to the next book!

E.G. Stone is an independent author who has been writing, creating and causing vast amounts of trouble since the age of six. Since then, E.G. has improved rather a lot in both the trouble-causing and writing and now spends her time writing fantasy and science fiction. When not writing, she is off musing about the workings of languages, both real and created, or drawing and sewing. E.G. reads voraciously, perhaps to the point of slight-insanity. Weird, nerdy, perhaps a little crazy, she is having a grand old time writing, reading, reviewing, interviewing, and, naturally, continuing her endeavours in causing trouble.